# THE TROUBLE
# WITH PARADISE

ALSO BY DAVID A. ROSS

*XENOS*:
*A romantic novel of travel and self-discovery*
*in the Grecian Isles*

# THE TROUBLE WITH PARADISE

David A. Ross

Published by ESCAPE MEDIA, 1998.
Denver, Colorado

Library of Congress Catalog Card Number: 97-94723

ISBN: 0-9661861-0-9

Front and back cover photos Copyright 1998 by Escape Media
Author's photo: Claudine Ross

First Escape Medial printing January 1998.
Second printing November 1998.
Third printing October 1999.

*WITH LOVE AND GRATITUDE, FOR CLAUDINE,*
*LIFELONG PARTNER IN THIS*
*GRAND ADVENTURE*

PART I.

Chapter 1.

"WE ARE ON THE LINE OF POSITION 157 DASH
337. WILL REPEAT THIS MESSAGE. WILL REPEAT THIS
MESSAGE ON 6210 kcs. WAIT/LISTENING ON 6210. WE
ARE RUNNING NORTH AND SOUTH."

Leaning forward into the stick, the pilot pointed the nose
of her Lockheed *Electra dural*, NR 16020, downward and guided
the plane through a dense layer of cumulus clouds. Within a thick
mass of gray vapor she flew blindly for several minutes, the peace
of a surreal aerial world broken only by the steady roar of the
plane's twin Pratt & Whitney engines.

Emerging from an opaque mist at seven hundred feet, AE
drew a concerned breath and turned to her navigator. "We should
be in visual range by now, Freddy. But I don't see it."

Having crawled from the cramped quarters of the
fuselage into the flight cabin, the navigator, too, searched the
expanse of steely water below. Since they'd turned eastward
somewhere near Truk Island, he had tried to take a star fix. To
no avail. And after several unsuccessful attempts to penetrate the
cloud cover at thirteen thousand feet, he was reduced to dead
reckoning in darkness to establish a heading.

3

At first light they broke through the clouds for a few minutes and he was able to determine a sun line with the sextant. Yet now the tiny Pacific island where they were supposed to land was not to be found.

"Keep to the present course," he instructed without alarm. "We're close now."

"I've been on the short wave trying to locate the *non-directional beacon*," the pilot related. "I was hoping we'd have a sighting when we came through this break in the clouds. The visibility is lousy. No telling how far the clouds and fog extend."

Amelia mentally recounted the US Fleet Air Base weather news received just before take-off from the airport at Lea, New Guinea: FORECAST THURSDAY, LEA TO ONTARIO. PARTLY CLOUDY, HEAVY RAIN SQUALLS TWO HUNDRED FIFTY MILES EAST OF LEA. WIND EAST SOUTHEAST, TWELVE TO FIFTEEN. ONTARIO TO LONGITUDE ONE SEVEN FIVE, PARTLY CLOUDY, CUMULUS CLOUDS ABOUT TEN THOUSAND FEET, MOSTLY UNLIMITED. WIND EAST NORTHEAST EIGHTEEN. THENCE TO HOWLAND, PARTLY CLOUDY, SCATTERED HEAVY SHOWERS, WINDS EAST NORTHEAST FIFTEEN. AVOID TOWERING CUMULUS AND SQUALLS BY DETOURS AS CENTERS FREQUENTLY DANGEROUS.

"How's our fuel holding out?" the navigator wanted to know.

"We've used more than expected," she told him. "And right from the start wind speeds have been much stronger than forecasted. I'm guessing twenty-five to thirty. Avoiding storm centers spent fuel, and even though I made regular fuel transfers from the storage tanks to the wing-mounted gravity tanks..." She sighed in quandary and bit her lower lip. "The autogiro should have kept us on course while I was priming that infernal '*wobble*' pump. My forearm is aching. Maybe the manual pump isn't working properly."

"I've never trusted Sperry's autogiro," the navigator complained sourly. "Sure, it's good for keeping close to the

4

intended course, but it can't compensate for even minimal wind drift! One slight change in velocity or direction, and we're out here trying to find a pimple on the backside of an elephant. But don't worry, I'm certain that ribbon of runway FDR built for you is down there somewhere," he reassured.

"If you have any suggestions, Freddy, I'm listening."

"How much time do we have?"

"Thirty to forty minutes - that's all."

"What about the Coast Guard Cutter, *Itasca?*"

"It's supposed to be in the vicinity. I've been in contact, but reception is patchy at best. I'll try to raise them again."

The pilot began another transmission: "ITASCA, WE ARE ABOUT 100 MILES OUT/PLEASE TAKE BEARING ON US AND REPORT."

The response was garbled and full of static: "CANNOT TAKE BEARING ON 3105/PLEASE SEND ON 500, OR DO YOU WISH TO TAKE BEARING ON US/GO AHEAD PLEASE."

"On which frequency are you signaling?" the navigator questioned.

"I switched from 6210 kcs. to 3105 kcs."

"Without a trailing wire our range is limited," he consternated. "But that shouldn't be a problem this close in. Still, you've gotta stay with the pre-arranged frequency!"

Unable to completely understand *Itasca's* instructions, AE radioed once again: "KHAQQ CALLING ITASCA/WE MUST BE ON YOU BUT CANNOT SEE YOU/GAS IS RUNNING LOW."

"WE HEAR YOU ON 3105/MESSAGE OKAY/SENDING AAA's ON..."

"What are they saying? Can you make it out?" Amelia asked her navigator.

"Too much static," he said. "Keep trying."

"ITASCA WE ARE CIRCLING BUT CANNOT HEAR YOU/GO AHEAD ON 7500."

"AAAAAAAAAAAA/GO AHEAD ON 3105."

5

"KHAQQ CALLING ITASCA/WE RECEIVED YOUR SIGNALS BUT UNABLE TO GET A MINIMUM/PLEASE TAKE BEARING ON US AND ANSWER 3105."

"YOUR SIGNALS RECEIVED OKAY... IMPRACTICAL TO TAKE BEARING ON 3105 ON YOUR VOICE."

Like impossible legends, the towering clouds were reflected in Amelia's flight goggles. Fatigue and frustration showed on her face. Pressing chapped lips and closing her burning eyes for a single moment, she hoped that once she opened them she might see not the everlasting icon of sky and ocean, but the newly constructed landing strip at Howland. And having lived her life on the cusp of expectation, desire, belief, and luck, there was, at this point, little choice but to acknowledge, for pilot and navigator alike, that the future remained suspended on something so intangible as currents of air.

"I'm sending a series of long dashes over five seconds," she told Freddy Noonan.

"Look," the navigator reasoned, "I've done my best! After all the detours last night, it's amazing that we're as close as we are. And we have a sun line! So there's no reason we should be lost. I know Howland is down there!"

Three weeks prior to departure Noonan had implored her to install a trailing wire, warning her over and over again about the danger of becoming lost and disoriented over the Pacific. But she'd obstinately resisted the inclusion of a simple device that might have enabled them to broaden the band of short wave reception fourfold. "In all my years of flying," she persisted, "I've never used my radio, except to break the boredom with a little music!"

Now, uneasy in the reality of her navigator's portent, Amelia busied herself with a perfunctory check of the *Electra's* instruments. They were flying at an altitude of only seven hundred feet, due Northeast, at an air speed of one hundred forty miles per hour. Oil pressure was one hundred ninety-five pounds per square inch starboard, one hundred ninety port, and the

6

internal temperature of each engine was within acceptable limits. It was the fuel gauge that threatened an insoluble problem!

Focusing upon the barely discernible horizon, (gradients of light upon the water sometimes made it difficult to distinguish a land mass from a bank of clouds), the pilot continued to search for the landing site. Above the drone of the 500 horsepower 'Wasp' engines she could hear the short wave set hiss and crackle and make that curious tuning sound that seemed utterly nebulous one minute, and full of promise the next. She watched in silence as her navigator compared readings from each of his three compasses: one magnetic; one aperiodic; and the third a directional gyro. Concentrating intensely, he recorded readings from the *Electra's* newly installed, though sometimes unreliable, drift indicator. Furnished with up-to-the-minute information, he referred once more to his charts.

In spite of Freddy's unquestioned expertise as a navigator, (the success of Pan Am's early survey flights across the Pacific Ocean was due to a large extent on Noonan's development of aerial navigational techniques), his growing reputation as a drinker - not wholly undeserved - had slammed certain doors in the world of commercial aviation squarely in his face. Not to mention arousing caution on more personal fronts. Amelia knew that Freddy felt as though he'd been black-balled unfairly. By no means was he keeping his disdain to himself, and he always said he didn't give a damn about what most of his colleagues thought of him. Except for her. She sensed that. And like herself, she knew also that he loved to fly for the unbridled joy of it. For the sheer fun of it! Just to fly, and fly, and fly...

Amelia first experienced the ecstasy of flight at the age of eighteen and was immediately captivated. The road to esteem had been both long and difficult, but over time she won respect as an aviator and an iconoclast.

Years earlier, she'd been recruited as the first woman to cross the Atlantic non-stop. Probably the best overall pilot on board the 'Friendship', she was never permitted to fly the plane once they left Nova Scotia. In disappointment she spent the crossing lying on her belly in the rear cabin - at least until the exhausted pilot over-shot their projected landing site in Ireland by nearly a hundred miles. It was she who finally executed a perfect water landing in the fog at Burry Port, Wales, though the truth of the matter was long concealed.

First in Wales, then at the beautiful Southampton estate of the brilliant and gracious Lady Astor, the now celebrated crew of the Friendship was given the royal treatment by the Brits. "My dear girl, your sense of daring leaves us all rather breathless," Lady Astor told her. "Nevertheless, I believe I still would prefer to cross the Atlantic by ship. The truth is that I have no real interest in aviation," she declared.

Still, that intensely scrutinized flight, as well as the subsequent reception and many forthcoming accolades, was hardly the apex of her career in aeronautics. Flying from Long Island to LA over the checkerboard fields of mid-America, she would often land her single engine *Vega* right on Main Street of one dusty farm town or another. Upon seeing her plane touch down, farmers, shopkeepers, and their wives and children, would come running from their fields, or out of their stores and houses, welcoming her and offering food and lodging.

Whether she was traversing mid-America or flying non-stop from Honolulu to Oakland, G.P. was inevitably waiting for her at journey's end. Decidedly in his element, he entertained groups of overly-eager publicity people, or pandered to their current group of financial backers.

Of course she'd not turned to aviation for financial opportunity; she would have worn rags just to stay in the air. But with G.P. handling the details of business such sacrifices were hardly necessary, for her husband had natural genius when it came to public relations. The mundane tasks he asked her to perform, cogent to fund-raising - interviews, autograph signings, and the like - were often tedious, but she supposed it was a small effort to make for solvency. Worthy airplanes were prohibitively expensive. She now recalled the staged conversation that had taken place between herself and G.P. just prior to her departure.

Putnam: Tell me dear, why are you going on this trip?

8

The Pilot: G.P., you know it's because I want to.

Putnam: Well, how about taking me along?

The Pilot: Of course I think a great deal of you, but on a flight one hundred eighty pounds of gasoline might be a little more valuable.

Putnam: You mean you prefer one hundred eighty pounds of gasoline to one hundred eighty pounds of husband?

The Pilot: I think you guessed right.


To her chagrin, such contrived farewell scenes were always conducted in public view. Once again she'd delivered her lines on cue, without spontaneity or conviction, and feeling as though she'd been made to face too many lenses. Over time George Putnam's publicity effort had managed to remake her into some sort of weird iconographic representation. But her unwavering self-confidence gave her determination, and not even G.P.'s unflagging attempts at control and manipulation could put a crack in such a foundation.

Her thoughts turned to her longtime friend and confidant, Eugene Vidal, a high-level administrator in Roosevelt's Commerce Department.

"Wouldn't it be wonderful to just go off and live on a tropical island?" she had once fantasized to him. She then described in intricate detail how one might meet the difficulties of such a self-imposed exile.

Vidal knew her well - perhaps even better than George Palmer Putnam. He acknowledged that if any woman could survive the solitary, Spartan challenges of being marooned, surely it was her. Time and again he'd witnessed her singular focus and practical work ethic guide her over untried tides and currents, as famous aviatrix, pacifist, and feminist. And Vidal was aware of another side of her personality, the side that was whimsical and dreamy, and seldom expressed.

"You see anything yet?" Noonan asked, breaking her connection with the past.

"Are you kidding? In this fog it would be impossible to spot San Francisco, let alone Howland Island!"

"Anything on the short wave?"

"Nothing but static."

"We need to begin constructing a grid," Freddy advised. "We must be in the vicinity, so it's only a matter of dividing the area into sectors."

"It's a big ocean, Freddy," she said.

"How much time?" he asked as she banked right to begin the methodical search.

"Twenty minutes or so..."

As her eyes moved over the endless water, her thoughts returned to Gene Vidal. The evening before the flight had begun, they'd stood out on the tarmac together, talking. "What with the false start in Honolulu, and all the subsequent preparation, I'm totally exhausted," she confided to him. "Right from the beginning our financial backers have been putting on the pressure. I've decided this is going to be my last record-breaking flight, my swan song. You know, Gene, sometimes people just get tired of their own legends."

"What would G.P. say if he heard you talking like that?"

"Of course he'd say to me, 'Always think with your stick forward, darling!' But lately I've begun to feel as if I'm mortgaging the future."

"You'll pull it off. You've got to do it," Vidal cajoled. "What are futures for anyway?"

"Eugene, the truth is that you're only worried about the diminished prospects of the Ludington Line should I fail and be swallowed by the deep blue ocean."

Unable to take her sarcasm seriously, Vidal feigned a laugh and put his arm around her shoulder as they walked slowly toward the *Electra's* hangar. The red sun was now setting.

"When it comes to the future of commercial aviation your influence is going to be crucial, Amelia," he told her. "But you're more important than that to me. To all of us!"

"Maybe to you, Gene. To George? I'm not so sure. I've never really been sure..."

Flying north to south, then back again, the pilot created the grid her navigator had suggested. The delicate weave of her

10

pattern attempted to leave no area uninspected. Clouds and fog gathered below, threatening to engulf her plane. Again the pilot leaned into the stick, this time taking the *Electra* all the way down to five hundred feet.

"I can't see the ocean anymore, Freddy," she said.

Impressed by her steady comportment, the navigator watched as she moistened her weathered and cracking, heart-shaped lips with the tip of her tongue. Her sun-bleached, short hair had become dry and frangible, while her brows were golden from many hours spent in the cockpit beneath the blazing equatorial sun. On several occasions she'd told him she was *not* afraid to die; in fact, try as she might, she had never been able to envision herself growing old. Transfixed, Freddy painted a vivid portrait in his mind that might somehow endure personal oblivion. "Try the radio again," he said.

"WE ARE ON THE LINE OF POSITION 157 DASH 337/WILL REPEAT THIS MESSAGE ON 6210 kcs./WAIT, LISTENING ON 6210 kcs./WE ARE RUNNING NORTH AND SOUTH/WE ARE RUNNING ON LINE/WILL REPEAT..."

The pilot descended another two hundred feet and still fog inhibited a visual search. Somehow sensing its plight, the plane's starboard engine missed and knocked, as if the heart of exploration itself had skipped a beat.

Noonan looked up nervously, expectation written all over his sunburned face. He wanted to say something significant, to recap the myriad events of his life in a single word, but before he could utter a sound, the able pilot pulled out the choke, and the engine came roaring back to a measured equilibrium.

That was just like her, he thought, disarming disaster with a deft flick of her wrist, controlling the uncontrollable with her cool competence.

"I thought you told me we had enough fuel for twenty minutes," Noonan said.

"Measuring range is *not* an exact science, Freddy," she said to him.

"What do we do now?" he asked.

"I'm taking it down a little further," she informed.

Freddy could now see the foamy waves reflected in her blue-gray eyes. Her slender fingers clutched the stick with white-knuckled determination. Her body had gone rigid against disaster.

"We'll continue searching until we're out of fuel," she determined. "But if I have to ditch her in the ocean... Why don't you begin unfolding the rubber lifeboat, Freddy? But let's pray we don't need it..."

"Right!" he said as he crouched down to re-enter the fuselage. "And remember Eddie Rickenbacker!" he proclaimed.

Moments later, at one hundred feet and still flying blind, the fuel was exhausted and the stuttering engines shook the plane before coming to a halt. Rocking and diving, the *Electra* cut through the fog. The wings tipped, balance was lost, and they could both feel the vacuum of rapid descent.

"This is it, Freddy," she called out. "I'm afraid we're going down!"

Lost in terror and disbelief, the navigator said nothing, but clasped his hands and began praying.

The pilot whispered the defining lines of her own poetical legacy:

*"Merciless life laughs in the burning sun,*
*And only death intervenes, circling down..."*

Chapter 2.

*'Relax - it's just a planet...'*

That was the handwritten message at the bottom of a black and white photograph that hung on the wall of Song Cajudoy's Sunrise Cafe in Lahaina Town. The faded print was of a sun-browned, Oriental-looking fellow with a full face, long, black hair, a wispy little goatee, and a big smile on his lips. For some unexplainable reason Julian Crosby could not take his eyes off the picture.

He was also keenly interested in the girl working behind the counter. She was a *petite* Filipina with delicate but determined-looking features, and her silky, black ponytail hung down over her flower-print shirt all the way to her waist. Her hands were nimble, and she moved quickly, so like the sparrows and finches that flew from perches in the mango tree just outside the cafe's wide-open, double doorway.

Normally not a deliberate eater, Julian lingered over breakfast today, and before he'd drunk his coffee and finished eating his banana-nut muffin, a willowy blond with a volcanic figure, wearing a very revealing bikini and a buoyant expression, came sauntering into the diner. Obviously a friend of the Filipina,

13

she casually ordered a glass of passion fruit juice, then inquired, "Where's Kamehaloha this morning?"

For the first time in over a year Kamehaloha Kong was not sitting at the Sunrise as the day dawned over the mid-Pacific. It was *his* enigmatic smile that beamed down from the picture on the wall. Song Cajudoy shrugged her shoulders as she poured the drink.

"Our *friend* is sailing his boat from Shipwreck Beach to Lahaina Harbor," she said. "I think he wants to sell it."

"Next time you see him," implored the blond, "tell him there's a *haole* in town looking for him, okay?"

"Sure," Song agreed. Her unappreciative opinion of Kamehaloha Kong was based primarily upon the fact that he owed her money for meals eaten at the Sunrise.

From his corner table Julian Crosby eavesdropped on their conversation. Shamelessly he admired the bikini girl. As she turned to walk out of the cafe her shoulders rocked gently and her long arms swayed like palm fronds touched by the Trades. Julian allowed that she was probably no older than his grown daughter, Kirsten.

He paid his bill and needlessly left a tip. Out the door and onto Front Street he wandered, past the Pioneer Inn and the giant banyan tree, all the way to the far end of the pier where the Carthaginian sailing ship was docked. There he stood out on the launch, watching rays of golden sunlight dance over the straight that separated Maui from Lanai Island.

Julian took a moment to acknowledge his broker, Kevin Miles, who had first suggested, then facilitated this Maui vacation. "So you were right about this place, my friend. Here a decrepit attitude doesn't stand a chance for survival..."

Julian spent most of the morning exploring the leeward side of the West Maui Mountains. Driving through the cane fields after noon he stopped at a busy farmer's market in Wailuku to buy mangoes and a pineapple, then drove *mauka* to Pukulani and Makawao, where Hawaiian *paniolos* worked on upcountry ranches. Later, on the ninth floor balcony of Miles' ocean-view condo, he cooked *ahi* on a gas barbecue and assembled a salad

14

made from tropical fruits. He drank an entire bottle of Chardonnay to toast his arrival in Hawaii.

The view from the lanai was sublime. Molokai Island appeared distant and surreal at sunset as the billowy clouds concealed its conical summit. Its leeward canyons were cast in fiery shades of pink and mauve. As dusk fell Julian heard the sound of waves breaking onshore. The white foam was oddly luminescent in near darkness. In the distance the 'Sugar Train' whistled as it chugged through the cane fields from Kaanapali to Lahaina Town.

The ocean breeze cooled the apartment, and Julian slept more soundly than he could remember sleeping in years. It was barely light when he opened his eyes. For a moment he lay in bed trying to recreate the fundamentals of a dream he was certain he'd dreamed. In time a curious image presented itself.

Sitting on a bridge near a rain forest waterfall was the round-bodied Hawaiian he'd seen in the photo at the Sunrise Cafe. With bare feet and busy hands the 'fruit juice philosopher' was weaving baskets out of freshly cut, vibrantly green palm fronds. Aware of the *haole's* intrusion he extended his thumb and little finger. "*Aloha*, brother!"

"*Aloha*," Julian returned the greeting.

"A little out of your element, aren't you?"

Julian shrugged. "I think everybody's looking for a little piece of paradise..."

"True, brother. But *Paradise* is surely a state of mind. Don't you agree?"

"Come on now," Julian wrangled. "Who could contend splendor like this?"

Of course he was referring to the many and obvious blessings of a prolific tropical garden - as well as to the mental and emotional comfort it so quickly and unanimously imparted.

"But the umbrage is quite dense, and maybe the *haole* doesn't truly understand," Kong said cryptically.

"What's a *haole*?" Julian asked. "I keep hearing the word, but I'm afraid I don't know it."

The Hawaiian laughed at him. "You are *haole*!"

15

"The blond girl at the Sunrise said we would meet."

"Could be we have important business," conjectured Kong.

"With all due respect," said Julian, "business is the furthest thing from my mind."

"A poor choice of words on my part, brother. No doubt, your trip is one intended for pure pleasure!"

"So where do you fit in?" Julian wanted to know.

Kamehaloha's big belly rolled. "Kahuna's power is very curious, brother. I search your soul. I uncover dreams and fantasies. Then I work through your sense of possibility. But such things are never precise."

"An accepted risk," acknowledged Julian.

"Like it or not, I'm the fly in your soup. It's my task to throw the world off its axis!"

"You don't say," said Julian skeptically.

The Chinese-Hawaiian busied his hands with his weaving. "Remember one thing, Julian. I never make knots which are impossible to untie!"

Again Julian heard the sound of the breakers rolling onshore, and redirecting his attention back to more tangible circumstances, he quickly dismissed the memory of a strange dream, already fading. Putting on his bathrobe he walked onto the lanai to assess the morning weather. A thin mantle of fog cloaked the velvety escarpments to the east. The sea was gray and foamy, bold but not cold-looking. Though it was quite early he observed a young couple making their way, arm-in-arm, up the deserted beach, and was momentarily overcome with the uneasy suspicion that too many opportunities had been missed, and good years gone by. How utterly absurd it suddenly seemed that he'd never run barefoot along the seashore. Determined to correct this omission immediately he put on his bathing suit and went downstairs to the beach.

One mile up and one mile down: he stopped periodically to examine his footprints left on the fine sand. They were not unlike the others he saw, but the waves washing onshore erased his telltale signature almost as quickly as he'd made it. He stopped to watch two wind surfers flying over eight-foot waves with their sails unfurled. He experienced a vicarious feeling of freedom, as if *he* were the one riding the thundering swells.

This ribbon of wind-swept beach separated the ocean from a life-size terrarium. Here blossoms of every conceivable shape and color - Birds of Paradise, Torch Ginger, Heliconia - engendered within Julian a reformed sense of personal size and proportion. Such a profusion shifted his attention away from the triviality of toil and replaced it squarely on the majesty of nature. Quite unconsciously he'd begun the unequivocal process of giving up a long-fostered, nervous and competitive perspective.

Walking inland he discovered a network of wondrous caves - cool, moist and mossy - where patches of ferns grew out of cracks in the rocks and water trickled down the walls into limpid cave pools. Peering into the depths he drew a startled breath and blinked his eyes in disbelief. Overcome with a sensation that he'd rediscovered a place both secret and taboo, Julian thought he saw the image of a beautiful girl - not Polynesian, but fair-skinned and Tutonic-looking - taking shape in the concentric ripples where his reflection should have appeared. Her cool, blue-gray eyes reflected a keen awareness of her circumstance and seemed to suggest mysteries beyond the realm of time. Her tensile body intimated both elemental conflict *and* natural harmony. She appeared to be endlessly searching some unfathomable horizon. Who was she?

Quite unaccustomed to revelation, Julian drew back.

Suspended between doubt and security, he returned to Kevin's Lahaina condo. There he bathed in the Jacuzzi for an hour, trying without much success to calm his newfound visionary predilection. That night he went to bed before it was fully dark.

Next morning he awoke early with the obscure feeling that he was late for an appointment. Considering he knew not a soul on Maui, such an impression seemed unfounded. Still the sensation would not leave him. And having eaten nothing the night before, he was very hungry, so he dressed and walked up Front Street to the only restaurant open at this hour - Song Cajudoy's Sunrise Cafe.

17

He ordered coffee and a cinnamon roll.  The only other customer in the cafe at this hour was the enigmatic local in the black and white photo - the same rain forest basket weaver of Julian's fantasy/dream!  With a glass of fruit juice before him, the *kahuna* meditated at one of the outdoor tables facing the sea, contemplating Hibiscus corollas on a trellis as he waited for the sunrise.

"Mr. Kong, my name is Julian Crosby," said the *haole*.

The Hawaiian nodded in recognition.  "Do you want to sit down?"

"Thanks," said Julian.  "The girl at the counter told me your name."

"Somebody said there was a *haole* looking for me."

"I heard you have a boat for sale."

"You want to buy a boat?"

"I've been considering it," Julian said.

"You don't look like a sailor," said Kamehaloha Kong.

"I'm not, really.  I sailed occasionally in California.  But that was awhile ago.  I decided to come over to Maui for an extended vacation, and my friend in San Diego generously offered me his condo.  And I've been thinking it might be great to get a boat.  Nothing too fancy - just big enough to go from island to island.  It's probably a foolish idea."

"Maybe the *best* reason to do it!" said Kong, wringing his thick hands and sermonizing.  "When you're young, brother, you pay a dime and get a dollar's worth of pleasure.  But when you get old, you pay a dollar and only get a dime's worth of fun.  How old are you, anyway?"

"I'm fifty-two," said Julian.

"So maybe you can get forty-five cents on a buck," Kong laughed.

"How big is your boat?" Julian asked.

"It's a six-passenger, thirty-one foot Bertram Flybridge Sportfisher called 'Scoundrel'.  It's powered by twin four-cylinder, one hundred sixty-five horse inboards.  It's a real beauty!  The engines are a little fickle if they're not tuned just right, but you'll get a feel for that.  No problem..."

18

"How much are you asking for it?" Julian wanted to know.

"Eighteen thousand cash," said Kong. "I'm probably giving it away, but these things have a funny way of coming back to you. Anyway, I'm hard up for money."

"When can I have a look?" Julian said, a little surprised at himself.

"What's wrong with right now?" said Kong. "It's docked in slip number thirteen over at the small boat harbor at the end of Canal Street. We can walk there in five minutes time."

Chapter 3.

Kamehaloha Kong tinkered with the Scoundrel's engines for nearly fifteen minutes before he was able to make them turn over, but finally the twin inboards rose to life with a roar that shattered the morning serenity in an ear-splitting, bone-rattling, two-cycle cacophony. The sound of the motors sent tremors of doubt thundering through Julian's uncertain sense of security, but the Hawaiian was able to adjust each choke until combustion was assured. He piloted the boat out of Lahaina Harbor as if it were an old friend.

Looking out to sea, Julian remarked idiotically, "That's a helluva lot of water..."

"Sure thing, brother," laughed Kamehaloha Kong. "And that's just the top of it!"

The captain turned his boat starboard and began paralleling Maui's western coastline. He steered the craft past Maalaea Harbor, Kihei, Wailea Resort, and Makena, Maui's southernmost point. Well away from shore, he opened up the throttle and powered the cruiser over the incoming waves.

Standing on deck and holding tightly to the side railing, Julian tried to look nautical, but in actuality looked weak and forlorn and more than a little out of place. The biting sea spray made his office-white face tingle, and the wind plastered his hair straight back. But he was not cold, for the Trades kept the temperature moderate day and night.

"What do you think?" Kamehaloha called down from his position on the head.

"It has plenty of spirit," Julian observed.

"Do you want to take the wheel?" Kong asked.

"Maybe after a while. I'm not sure I have my sea legs yet."

"I'm heading around the southern shore to Molkini Island," Kong declared.

"Wherever you want to go," Julian acceded, "I'm with you!"

In Molokini's sunken crater, calm, clear waters were almost guaranteed for novices and experienced divers alike. Kamehaloha Kong turned off the engines and dropped anchor near the crescent-shaped, volcanic islet. He made no immediate attempt to explain his intentions to Julian, but descended to the main deck and popped open a storage compartment which housed an impressive array of scuba equipment. "Have you ever made a dive?" he asked.

"I'm afraid I've not had the pleasure," said Julian dubiously.

"It's pretty easy," said Kong without concern. He began pulling various pieces of equipment out of the compartment. "I have expert classification. I'll give you a little instruction and have you suited up in a matter of minutes."

"Really?" said Julian.

"Hey! No problem, brother."

Julian dressed down to his swimming trunks, and Kamehaloha Kong lifted a light-weight backpack apparatus with protruding hoses, gauges, and straps onto Julian Crosby's shoulders. He adjusted the position of a single air tank before the neophyte could lodge a protest, and with a large-lipped, toothy smile on his big face, he initiated a crash course.

"This jacket is your *buoyancy compensator*," Kamehaloha explained. By inflating it with just the right amount of air one could maintain stasis under water, he explained. Air was added by blowing into a ribbed tube. It was released with a valve. "You see?" he asked. Kong repeated the demonstration so any fool might comprehend the procedure.

Julian looked overwhelmed.

"And here's your *regulator*," Kong continued. "Put it in your mouth and breath naturally. There's really nothing to it." He then showed Julian how to read the crucial gauges measuring ocean depth and air tank pressure.

"Now put on your fins and spit in your mask," he told him. "That'll keep it from fogging up. Once we're in the water, hold your nose and blow the pressure out of your ears. And stay with me no matter what happens. We'll descend very slowly down to fifty or sixty feet. When it's time to come up, follow your slowest air bubble to the surface and you won't get the bends."

"Are you sure I can do this?" Julian appealed.

But his supplication was already too late as Kamehaloha took him by the arm and jumped overboard.

Truly, unique experiences had never been Julian Crosby's passion, and he now found himself wondering why he'd allowed Kamehaloha Kong to maneuver him into such a situation. Yet he could not deny the novelty of this experience. A once abstract and anomalous world now tolerated him as an alien guest!

On the surface was a great light; he could almost feel the intensity of some luminary beacon shafting through the water. Below, against a backdrop of ever-deepening shades of green and gray, lay the vast coral reef and sandy bottom. Myriad schools of multicolored, tropical fish, (supported by a grand and diverse cast of undersea plants pulsating to the rhythms and currents of the fluent medium), brought the mercurial art of water ballet to its natural zenith. And simply putting on a mask had unveiled this silent world which appealed to some primordial atom deep within his ancient consciousness.

Along the coral reef the crystalline framework of the radically symmetrical bodies - brittle tentacles of calcium carbonate - formed a gorgonian colony: orange and purple sea

22

feathers; fans; calcareous spicules with erect central rods surrounded by conglomerate cylinders. Prolific were the hydras, jellyfish, and sea anemones. There were mollusks and snails and crabs. A Crown-of-thorns, a Spiny Sea Urchin, a Diadema, a Gall crab... Julian became entranced by the parade of fishes: first a Parrotfish swam right in front of him; followed by a Lionfish with its colorful, zebra-like patterns. A shoal of Jewelfish awash in chromium-pink, changing to silvery-yellow in reflective light, was no more than an arm's length away.

Kamehaloha directed Julian's attention to a vibrant stand of fire coral. Waving his hand from side to side, he instructed the novice diver not to touch the poisonous branches. Then he pointed out a community of Moray eels, green and snake-like with geometric patterns which, themselves, appeared to be undulating as the creatures slithered inquisitively near the reef's foundation.

In this esoteric world of intricate patterns and temporal networks, linear measurement lost all meaning, and Julian now floated in an odd state of suspension. So when Kong pointed to his watch and motioned toward the surface, Julian was surprised to learn that they had already been diving for nearly and hour. They ascended slowly, Crosby at Kong's heels, so the pressure could equalize within their bloodstreams. As they neared the surface the light of day grew brighter and brighter. Suddenly they were above water, and for a moment the world of dry land and air felt curiously foreign to Julian.

Onboard the Scoundrel, Julian was all expletives.

"What an experience! That was fantastic! I never imagined it would be so..." He fell speechless.

"So you liked it," said Kong as he peeled off his mask and began unfastening his *BC*. "I knew if I told you what I had in mind you would have put up some kind of fight. Now you're aware of something new."

Still dripping sea water, Julian sat on the Scoundrel's deck. Considerable suction was created between the rubber fins and bare skin, and a popping sound punctuated their conversation as he peeled off his flippers.

"This was probably some sort of tactic to make me want to buy the boat," said Julian. "And perhaps it was successful..."

"You think you want to buy it?" Kong asked as he wrung water from his long hair.

"On two conditions," said Julian, still breathless.

"What conditions?"

"That you include the two scuba outfits. And that we spend another day sailing together so I can become thoroughly familiar with every operation on board."

"Okay," said the Hawaiian. Kamehaloha's characteristic smile spread over the breadth of his brown face. Julian, too, beamed at the notion of owning the Scoundrel.

"We can sail over to the Big Island next Sunday," Kong suggested. "I hear there's going to be a *luau* at Hilo Harbor. We shouldn't miss it, Julian. You can drop me off there, then go anyplace the Scoundrel will take you. I have only one more question."

"What's that?" Julian asked.

"Do you have eighteen thousand in cash?"

Julian paused for a moment as he looked the Hawaiian directly in the eye. "I can get it," he said. "But you'll have to give me a couple of days to have the money transferred to a Hawaiian bank."

"I think the *haole* just bought himself a boat," said Kong, extending his hand. "Congratulations, brother!"

And they shook hands to seal the agreement.

Chapter 4.

In January 1937, Amelia Mary Earhart Putnam stood in the doorway of the Round Robin Lounge off the lobby of the venerable Willard Hotel in Washington, D.C. Having just come from the salon, and dressed in a new, smart-looking blue suit with a silk scarf, a black belt and bag, pumps, and her silver *Distinguished Flyer's Cross*, she searched the room for her longtime friend, Eugene Vidal, but did not locate him.

Approaching her, the *Maitre d'hotel* bowed graciously. "May I be of service, Miss Earhart?"

By now she probably should have been accustomed to being recognized, yet such familiarity in public still managed, time and again, to catch her off guard.

"I'm meeting a friend, Mr. Eugene Vidal. But perhaps he's not here yet," she speculated.

"Mr. Vidal is seated at the back of the room," he told her. "By his request," he added. "Please allow me to escort you, Miss Earhart."

At Vidal's table the host withdrew. Gene stood up and kissed her lightly on the cheek, then pulled out her chair. "Welcome to Washington, AE," he said as they sat down.

"It's dreadfully cold here," she remarked.

"What do you expect? It's January!"

"I'm acclimated to the weather in California," she said.

"How's George?" Vidal asked.

"Feeling sour about not being included for the White House luncheon." She smiled indulgently at the minor tantrum G.P. had thrown before she left Oakland.

Knowing George Putnam's moods, Vidal chuckled. "I'm sure he'll get over it," he said.

A waiter arrived to take their drink orders. Though it was just before noon, Vidal ordered a scotch and soda; AE wanted only tonic water.

"You must admit," she conjectured, "it's a little odd that G.P. was not invited."

"Not if you know the Roosevelts," said Vidal.

"Mrs. Roosevelt has always been totally supportive of my flying," she told him.

"The First Lady is captivated by you, Amelia."

"Don't tell me things like that, Gene. I'm nervous enough about this luncheon."

"Why?" he wanted to know. "You've been to the White House before. You've met the president and Mrs. Roosevelt."

"But not for lunch in their private quarters. What do you suppose this is all about?"

"Part of Roosevelt's charm is the way he perpetuates mystery," imparted Vidal. "So what's today's protocol?"

"The limousine is picking me up in an hour," she related. To Vidal, AE seemed uncharacteristically nervous as she took a compact from her bag and checked her already flawless make-up.

During the next forty-five minutes they discussed ongoing repairs by Lockheed to the *Electra* following the aborted take-off and roll-over in Honolulu. Amelia told him that the repairs were going well and that as a result of the accident several innovations were being incorporated into the plane's structure. They also discussed plans to establish, following the completion of her equatorial flight, a new commercial airline.

"Of course you know that Harry Manning's withdrawn as navigator for the around-the-world flight," she said to Eugene.

" I didn't know that. Since when?"

"Since we returned from Hawaii. He says it's because his leave of absence will run out before we can get underway again, but I think it's something more - something personal."

"Involving you or G.P.?"

She took a sip of the tonic then dabbed her lips with the cocktail napkin. "I can't determine," she said. "But it looks as though I'm going to have to find another navigator."

"That's unfortunate," said Vidal. "Who do you have in mind?"

"G.P. wants Freddy Noonan. But I don't know."

"Freddy's a great navigator, of course. But if those rumors about why he was sacked by Pan Am are true..."

"What do you mean *if* they're true? Gene, everybody knows Freddy has a problem with booze."

"So why even consider him, Amelia?"

"Because when he's sober there's nobody better."

"Sounds risky," said Vidal.

Amelia smiled ironically. "The entire flight is risky."

At twelve forty-five the *Maitre d'hotel* approached their table: "Sorry to intrude, Miss Earhart," he apologized, "but the limousine has arrived to take you to the White House."

Amelia patted Vidal on the shoulder. "Can't keep the president waiting," she said.

"Of course not..." He smiled at her.

She was escorted out of the lounge, through the elegant lobby, and out the revolving doors. There a White House chauffeur stood holding the door of the limousine open for her. She slid inside, the driver closed the door, and they were off to Sixteen Hundred Pennsylvania Avenue.

Arriving at the White House by one-fifteen, Amelia was shown directly upstairs to the living quarters of the First Family. In a marble-white foyer, Mrs. Roosevelt welcomed her cordially and told her, "My dear, Amelia, you always look so full of vitality. You're truly amazing. Truly..."

"Thank you, Mrs. Roosevelt," AE blushed.

27

"We're so happy you could come to luncheon today. We know you must be incredibly busy with preparations for your upcoming flight. I don't know how you do it, dear. We so admire your courage. Now, please don't be bashful. Come into our little parlor and say hello to Franklin. I know he's anxious to talk with you."

As the First Lady took her by the hand and led her into their private parlor - a lavish yet still homey room - Amelia saw the president sitting comfortably on a divan, his crutches nearby. A second man sat nearby the president - middle-aged, square-shouldered, and well dressed - though AE's attention was naturally drawn to FDR.

Roosevelt's complexion was florid, and his partially gray hair was a little out of place, as though he might have been having a cat nap just prior to the guests' arrival. Holding a lighted cigarette in a filigreed holder, he looked at her over the top of his Nez-perce glasses.

"Amelia Earhart!" he boomed.

This man, this president, had a distinctive way of making whomever he was addressing at the moment feel like the most important person he would see all day long. Amelia had met him before, and she liked him very much. One could not help liking FDR! And Mrs. Roosevelt was delightful!

"It's good to see you again, Mr. President," she said, moving across the room, then shaking hands with deference. "Thank you for inviting me to the White House."

"The pleasure is ours," he said with a captivating smile. "Eleanor and I think the world of you, young lady. Imagine how many young people - especially little girls - are inspired by your accomplishments!"

"I simply do what I do," Mr. President. "I fly because I love it!"

"The best reason to do anything, I suspect," said FDR. He removed his cigarette from its holder and dashed it out in a nearby ash tray, then turned toward his other guest. "Please allow me to present Mr. James Forrestal, Undersecretary of the

28

United States Navy." He turned back to Amelia. "James, may I present Mrs. Amelia Earhart Putnam."

Forrestal stood up and offered his hand to Amelia. "The honor is all mine, Mrs. Putnam," he said. "I've followed your career with great interest."

"My husband sees to it that my so-called exploits are well publicized," she explained with humility.

"Amelia's husband is George Putnam, the publisher," Eleanor offered.

Forrestal nodded his recognition. Amelia looked over at the president, who was smiling.

"Shall we move to our little dining room?" suggested Mrs. Roosevelt. "I believe they're ready to serve lunch."

"Splendid," said the president. "I'm hungry!" he declared. He reached for his crutches and struggled to stand upon braced legs. Though several aids waited nearby, no one moved to assist him, for they'd long ago been instructed as to his preference for independence.

The Roosevelt's dining room combined the formality of the White House with the imported personal comforts of Hyde Park. The table and chairs were Chippendale - not overly large or intimidating. Above a credenza hung a genuine Winslow Homer. The large window opposite the double doorway looked out upon a snowy west lawn surrounded by bare trees.

The dining table itself was laid with fine white linens monogrammed in silver thread. Four silver candlesticks with tapered white candles were placed round a floral centerpiece of lilies. The china was Doulton, and the crystal water goblets were etched with the Presidential Seal. FDR sat at the head of the table; Eleanor opposite him. Amelia was seated at the president's right, and Mr. Forrestal at his left.

After crab cocktails and spinach salads, they were served Filet Mignon, saffron rice, buttered limas, and baby carrots. For dessert they were offered lemon chiffon cake. Over coffee the president nodded for the servers to leave the room, then asked Amelia how the repairs to her airplane were progressing.

"Quite well," she told him. "But it's terribly expensive. The *Electra* was not insured, you know. No company was willing to assume the risk. But we're hoping to be ready for a second try by the beginning of June."

"That soon?" said FDR.

"If we can raise the funds. Though we've decided to reverse our course," she explained. "Instead of flying east to west, we'll be traveling west to east."

"Why is that?" inquired Mr. Forrestal.

"Global weather patterns have changed since our first attempt," she told him.

"Then you'll be flying over the Pacific at the end of your journey?"

"Right," said AE.

"You know," said FDR, "we're beginning to hear disquieting news concerning Japanese activities in the mandates."

"I don't understand," said Amelia.

"After the War," explained the president as he placed a cigarette in his holder, "the League of Nations mandate prohibited all military activity in the South Pacific. Of course, the Japanese have now withdrawn from the League of Nations. I have information from personal sources - French, not American - that the Japs have ignored the mandate and are building oil storage tanks in the Carolines and the Marshall Islands. Shells for three-inch guns were seen being unloaded from supply ships - concrete airplane ramps, hangars, entire machine shops... Word is out that they're dredging the harbor at Jaluit Island in order to make it navigable for big supply ships. When our own ships tried to call at Mili atoll, we were turned away. Apparently, there's something very sensitive going on out there..."

Forrestal offered FDR a light.

"What do you presume their intentions to be, Mr. President?" Amelia boldly asked.

The president took a reflective puff of his cigarette. "Amelia, you must understand," he explained, "that our own intelligence-gathering agencies are radically under funded. I complain until I'm blue to the various appropriations committees,

30

but, in truth, there's not much I can do to influence the isolationists. Even if *they* can nurture a little ignorance, as president, *I* can't afford such complacency. One way or another, I must know what's going on out there."

Forrestal was next to speak: "I'd like to know, Mrs. Putnam, just what is the range of your modified aircraft?"

Amelia's expression showed the confidence she felt in the plane she'd recently received from Purdue University.

"Lockheed Corporation has done a marvelous job of designing and installing extra fuel tanks in the fuselage," she told Forrestal. "In theory, the *Electra* can carry over eleven hundred gallons of fuel. But it's doubtful I'd ever get off the ground with such a weight load. Still, with nine hundred fifty-four gallons, I was able to fly non-stop from Oakland to Honolulu, and on arrival there was plenty of gas in reserve. Presumably, the plane has a range of four thousand miles, though such a flight would have to be made in near perfect conditions. And such conditions exist only in theory, not in practice."

"So, it will not be possible for you to fly all the way from Asia to the Hawaiian Islands without refueling," Forrestal concluded.

"Quite correct," said Amelia. "It will be necessary to refuel somewhere between Papua New Guinea and the Hawaiian archipelago."

"Have you determined a refueling point yet?" he asked.

"I'm afraid we haven't completed the flight plan. My husband has made inquiries to Naval authorities about the possibility of refueling in mid-air over Guam, and they've been quite encouraging. But a far better target might be Howland Island."

"Where's that?" FDR wanted to know.

Forrestal reached into his brief case and brought out a US Navy hydrographic map of the South Pacific. He laid the map out in front of the president and pointed out the spec of land in question. "It's right here, Mr. President. Just south and east of the Marshalls."

"There's only one problem," said Amelia.

"What's that?" Roosevelt wanted to know.

"There's no runway there."

The president stroked his chin in thought. He took off his glasses and began cleaning them with his handkerchief. "Perhaps your friend, Mr. Vidal, might be of some help," he suggested.

"I don't understand," said Amelia. "How might Eugene help?"

"Well, considering our need for intelligence in the region, I believe certain funds in DOC might be made available for such a project."

"Mr. President, are you suggesting that Eugene Vidal build me an airstrip on Howland Island?" Amelia asked incredulously.

"Franklin only wants to insure your success, my dear," said Mrs. Roosevelt.

"The *Electra* will need about fifteen hundred feet," the aviatrix postured.

"I'm sure that won't pose any problem," said FDR casually.

"I don't know what to say," Amelia blushed. "If there is something I might do..."

"Young lady, you've proven yourself time and again to be a credit to your country," said FDR as he finished his coffee and dashed out his cigarette butt. "Still, there *is* a service you might perform for me in return for your runway," negotiated the president.

AE sat attentively. For the President of the United States was about to ask her for a personal favor. "Of course I'll try my best to be of whatever service..."

Forrestal moved the hydrographic map closer to the pilot. "Look here!" he addressed her. "If you were to leave Papua New Guinea around noon, you could be over the Carolines before dark, couldn't you?"

Amelia studied the naval map with interest. "Though it's not the most direct course to Howland, I suppose I could," she said.

"Truk Island is the one we're particularly concerned about," said Forrestal, dead serious.

"I presume it's Japanese territory," she said.

"Yes, it is," said Forrestal.

"And you'd like me to..."

"Photographs, Mrs. Putnam. We need rock hard evidence of ongoing military operations, but *we* can't get near them. You're another matter altogether! Thanks to your husband's efforts at publicity, the entire world is aware of your upcoming attempt to circumnavigate the globe at the equator. A few degrees off course is an error easily explained."

"So I would be spying."

"Does the idea give you nerves?" asked Forrestal.

Considering her history and accomplishments, such a notion seemed absurd. "Not particularly, sir."

But the undersecretary, too, was unflappable. He continued presenting the Government's proposition: "Might one also presume, Mrs. Putnam, that after turning east at Truk Island and flying all night, you would reach the Marshall Islands by daylight?"

With all the stakes on the table, Amelia was now inclined to play his game aggressively. She had always been good at gambling. "Yes, one might presume that, Mr. Forrestal," she said. "But remember, unless flying conditions are perfect, the *Electra* will be critically low on fuel as we turn south from the Marshalls and head for Howland Island."

"Of course this is speculative," reminded FDR.

"Of course," re-iterated the undersecretary.

"Look, Amelia," said the president earnestly, "I'm not one to pull punches. I need information. This is one way I can get it. I realize that such a mission is not without risk, but I also know that risk is your business! Some people handle risk well. You're one of those people. I trust you."

The profound implications of what the president was asking of her settled conclusively upon Amelia's consciousness. For in spite of the obvious hazard, (surely she did not wish to be captured as a spy by the Japanese), this *was* a duty she was willing to perform.

"Yes, I believe such a detour is possible, Mr. President," she nodded. "Of course my navigator will have to be thoroughly briefed."

"Who will be navigating?" asked Forrestal.

"We believe Fred Noonan is the best person for the job."

"Is Mr. Noonan likely to go along?" Forrestal wanted to know.

"I know that Freddy is intensely patriotic," Amelia related. "And I'm sure he'll consider it a privilege, as I do, to serve this office."

"I knew I could count on you, Amelia," said FDR. "Now, you must keep us informed on the progress of repairs to your plane. And if there's anything you need - anything at all..."

"Of course we'll have to work behind the scenes," said Forrestal. "I mean, it just wouldn't look right if we were out front on this."

"I understand," said Amelia. "I must say, I'm rather surprised. I thought was just coming to the White House for a casual luncheon. But I'm grateful for your interest, your trust, and of course your willingness to help."

With a self-satisfied look on his face, Roosevelt placed another cigarette in his holder. Forrestal leaned in close to flick his lighter. FDR nodded first at AE, then at Undersecretary Forrestal. A pact had been made.

Chapter 5.

The outrigger canoe rocked gently in the placid waters of the lagoon as the crew of the *Hawai'iloa* prepared for departure.

Not long ago the vessel's hulls had been tall trees. They had been felled, hollowed, and shaped with stone tools, then hand-polished with infinite care using small abrasive blocks of coral. The lashings were made from coconut fiber sennit rope, the sails from treated pandanus leaves.

Finally the navigator, Nainoa Nainoa, pulled away the prop which tethered the canoe to land, and the crew of rowers, standing waist-deep in the lagoon, vaulted joyously into the seventy-nine-foot hulls and took their positions on the moveable seats which slid back and forth within the craft's hollowed-out section.

With spume rising all about them and the tips receding back into darkened troughs, *Hawai'iloa* left the Marquesas and embarked upon its rightful journey. The unfurled sails sang in the favorable easterly wind as a lone canoe with thirty-three brave and seasoned sailors aboard rode over the combers and out to sea. Without compass they headed northward over the widest expanse of ocean on earth.

"Sail to the land guarded by 'seven little eyes'," called Nainoa Nainoa. Then he chanted an ancient prayer:

"Gods of the boundless deep,
Gods of the mighty waves
And troughs which lead to blackness,
We place our ship in your hands,
In your hands, our hopes and our lives."

\* \* \* \* \*

Julian Crosby now sat each morning at the Sunrise, sipping black Kona coffee, waiting for the eighteen thousand dollars to clear wire transfer, and hoping to catch one more glimpse of the willowy blond he'd seen at the cafe counter on his first morning in Lahaina.

The cafe's owner, Song Cajudoy, now recognized Julian's face, and today, for the first time, she ventured a personal question. "You here in Hawaii alone?"

"I'm flying solo these days," he nodded.

"I noticed your wedding ring. Where is your wife?"

"We were divorced a couple of years ago."

"But you still wear your wedding ring?"

Julian shrugged.

"I'm divorced, too," she confided. "My husband took all our money and went back to Manila. He left me here to work day and night at this lousy cafe. But I'd rather be in Hawaii. In the Philippines they close all the banks and tap the phone lines. Police beat everybody up for no good reason. Where's your wife now?"

"Living in Long Beach," Julian said.

"So, why divorce?" Song asked.

"I guess all the magic was gone," Julian said.

The Filipina nodded. "Magic is very, very important. Perhaps you've come to just the right place. What do *you* think?"

"Perhaps," conceded Julian.

36

"Listen!" said Song. "Today I make you omelet with special herbs. Maybe put some magic back in your life..."

"Why not?" said Julian.

Song smiled her delicate, Asian smile as she deftly cracked two brown eggs into a bowl, sprinkled in the promised herbs, and began beating the mixture with a wire whip.

And where was Kamehaloha Kong? Since their scuba diving lesson three days ago Julian had not seen him. Though he was certain Kong had not left the island. Each day Julian walked down to the boat launch to have another look at the Scoundrel, taking inventory of the cruiser from prow to stern. It was a fine boat, still he could not deny the buyer's remorse he was experiencing. In retrospect, he viewed the impulsive purchase as somewhat out of character. But perhaps he was becoming more inclined by the day to leave once rigid attitudes in his wake.

Maybe it was this place... What was the term Kevin had used? *Polynesian Paralysis.* That was it! Well, he was *not* paralyzed, that much was obvious. If anything, he was exercising self-direction for the first time in his life. Something had changed. Something important.

"Hey! Did you ever talk to Kamehaloha?"

Julian turned toward the voice. It was the blond.

"Yes, I agreed to buy his boat," he said.

"You bought the Scoundrel?" cawed Song Cajudoy as she brought his omelet to the table.

"It's a marvelous boat, don't you think so?"

"If you say so..." The cafe owner shook her head skeptically and said with sarcasm, "Now maybe he'll pay me what he owes me."

Well, Julian didn't know about that, but he was pleased to see that this beautiful girl - tall, strong and tan - whose image he'd not been able to put out of his mind since first seeing her at the Sunrise, was, for some unexplainable reason, interested in him - or at least in his impending purchase of the Scoundrel.

"We're sailing over to the Big Island on Sunday," he told her. "That'll give me an opportunity to get to know the boat a little better before I take it out alone. Apparently, there's some sort of ceremony taking place in Hilo that Kamehaloha wants to see." Julian took an anxious bite of the omelet as he stared at the girl; the eggs had a curious but compelling taste.

"Oh, the landing of *Hawai'iloa*, the voyaging canoe!" she exclaimed.

"What's that?" Julian wanted to know.

"You mean you don't know about the expedition?" Without being asked, she sat down at his table. "My name is Tamara Sly," she said.

"Julian Crosby. Pleased to meet you."

With full lips she sipped passion fruit nectar through a straw. Her sun-bleached hair fell capriciously over her cheeks and forehead. Her blue eyes were full of sun, too.

"I've only been in Hawaii a little more than a week," Julian explained. "What is this *expedition* all about?"

"*Hawai'iloa* is a modern-day re-creation of the voyaging canoes used by the ancient Polynesians," she explained. "For a long time it was thought that stories told by the Hawaiian priests were nothing more than myth and fantasy - that such a dangerous voyage was impossible without modern-day navigational equipment. Now, Nainoa Nainoa is attempting to make the trip navigating the old way - by the stars and other elements. They've been sailing for weeks, and they're due to land at Hilo this Sunday!"

"And that's what Kamehaloha wants to see..."

"It's a matter of intense cultural pride for the Hawaiian people."

"You're not a native Hawaiian," Julian observed.

"Hardly," she laughed. "I came here three years ago from Alaska. I guess you could say I was following the Trades."

"And what about Kamehaloha?"

"Hawaiian, through and through."

"But his last name is obviously Chinese."

She brushed her bangs aside, sat back, kicked off her sandals, and crossed her long, bare legs. "The first Chinese settlers came to Hawaii in the 1850's, I think. Mostly men. They worked on the sugar plantations and in the pineapple fields. They were incredibly frugal, and eventually they started their own businesses and bought land. Many of the immigrants married Hawaiian girls. Kamehaloha can trace his ancestry as far back as Sun Yat Sen, the Chinese revolutionary!"

"I guess I never realized Hawaiian genealogy was so complex," said Julian.

"Actually, there are very few full-blooded Hawaiians left. Most of them live on Ni'ihau, a tiny island off the west coast of Kauai. But *haoles* aren't allowed to go there."

"I keep hearing that word, *haole*," Julian said. "What does it mean, anyway?"

Tamara laughed. "You're *haole*! So am I. It's the Hawaiian word for non-Hawaiians, specifically Whites. It's an odd word, really. It comes from two words in their language: *Ha* means life; *ole* is death. The synthesis is something like living-dead."

"Sounds a little insulting," Julian ventured.

"Kamehaloha sometimes makes fun of *haoles*, but he's just a *local boy*. It's only talk; it doesn't mean anything. His heart is as big and bright as Haleakala!"

"He took me diving off Molikini Island the other day," Julian told her. "He seems like a terrific guy."

Eavesdropping on their conversation, Song Cajudoy coughed conspicuously at Julian's summation of Kamehaloha's personality.

"I know you're going to enjoy the Scoundrel," said Tamara. "And the landing of *Hawai'iloa* should be quite an event. I wish *I* were going to be there."

"Why not come along with us?" suggested Julian.

"You mean you wouldn't mind?"

"Why would I?" he said.

"I'd love to come," said Tamara. "Fill me in on all the details..."

Before the sun rose above Haleakala Crater, Julian arrived at Lahaina's small boat launch with a brand new attaché case filled with crisp one hundred dollar bills. Standing barefoot and alone on the pier where the Scoundrel was moored, he was inclined for a moment to question his sanity. Buying this boat seemed to imply some sort of unsuspected covenant.

Nevertheless, an idiosyncratic feeling of resignation overshadowed any lingering doubts, and inept as Julian might prove as a sailor, he was happy to be going to sea on his own boat. He hoped Tamara Sly would show up as planned for the trip to Hilo.

Sadly, Julian had begun to experience his own loneliness. It was not an unfounded sensation; rather it was a peculiar one which had long remained hidden and now surfaced at an unexpected time and place. He was making some rather eccentric friends here in Hawaii - not the safe sort of relationships to which he was accustomed. Kamehaloha Kong, Song Cajudoy, and Tamara Sly were colorful characters compared to his own thin-lined chiaroscuro, yet they seemed to accept him without condition.

Sleepy-eyed and fifteen minutes late, Kamehaloha appeared on the wharf wearing a T-shirt, baggy shorts, and flip-flops. He hadn't bothered to comb is overgrown hair, nor had he recently shaved. "*Aloha*, brother," he said to Julian, and patted him on the back with his thick hand.

"*Aloha*," Julian responded.

"Did the bank in San Diego send the cash?" the Hawaiian wanted to know.

Julian held up the attaché and confirmed, "Sure thing."

"Song told me you invited Tamara Sly to go with us this morning," he said.

"I hope it's okay," said Julian.

"It's your voyage, brother."

"How far is it to Hilo?" Julian asked as they went on board.

"About seventy-five miles, as the crow flies. It usually takes me two and a half to three hours, depending on the sea. I know it looks calm here in the harbor, but once we reach the *Na Pali* coast of the Big Island, there's no way to know."

Immediately they began making preparations to leave. Kong instructed Julian in the particulars of how to fuel the engines and adjust the two finicky carburetors, as well as how to raise anchor and back out of the slip. Before they were ready to cast off, Tamara Sly came sauntering up the pier. Though it was not yet seven o'clock and the sun was still behind the mountains, she was wearing her bikini overdraped by a sarong, rubber-soled sandals, and a pair of Raybans. She carried only a cloth over-the-shoulder bag. "What a beautiful morning!" she said as she came on board.

No less brightened by her presence, Julian thought. Not to mention his own revitalized fantasy. He bit his lower lip as she sat on deck, tossed her wavy, blond hair back, and crossed her slim legs.

Kamehaloha coaxed the engines to life and called to Julian, "Take the head, sailor boy!"

"Are you sure I should guide us out of the harbor?"

"You gotta learn sometime, brother."

Of course Kamehaloha was right, and Julian took the helm.

Slowly out of Lahaina Harbor they went in early morning: Julian Crosby, Kamehaloha Kong, and Tamara Sly. The water in the bay was calm, and Julian piloted the Scoundrel with the care of a new father handling his baby for the first time. Kamehaloha offered words of encouragement, as well as directions: "That's it, brother. Take it slow and easy. Around the reef you go. Once we're a few hundred yards offshore, you can open it up!"

The engines rumbled and coughed up dirty exhaust, while the foamy wash splashed against the ship's hull. At the head, in the captain's chair, Julian felt curiously at home in this less than familiar part.

Clearing the arc where the cruise ships were often moored, he pulled back on the throttle and felt the power of the twin inboards rise. His accumulated doubts and insecurities faded with the emergence of the tropical sun. And even before the deserted south shoreline of Maui was out of sight, the north shore

41

of the Big Island, with its twin snow-capped, volcanic peaks of Mauna Kea and Mauna Loa, came into view. Sheer, windswept cliffs, mantled in the delicate hues of a verdant rain forest, rose majestically from the tranquil sea. Great waves thundered against the rocky outcroppings and black sand beaches, ever changing the cast of the water from steely gray at its depths, to marine blue near the reef, to an intense shade of aqua in the lagoons, and finally to a foamy froth as it washed on shore. Around the northern apex of the archipelago's youngest island they sailed - past the wild and barely accessible Pololu Valley, along Hamakua Coast. There the ghosts and artifacts of Waipio Canyon offered stories of the ancient culture through one of its descendants, Kamehaloha Kong.

"This place looks peaceful now," related Kamehaloha, "but in ancient times there were sacrifices at the sacred *heiaus*. Many Hawaiians believe that along a section of Waipio Beach lies the entrance to the nether world. Ha! I suppose I believe it, too!" he laughed. "Once I was hiking at night with some friends through the canyon to the twin falls of Hiilawe, and in the long, moon lit shadows we saw a line of Night Marchers searching for the entrance to a secret domain." He looked provocatively at Julian. "Do you believe in spirits, brother?"

Julian drew a deep breath but said nothing. The dubious look on his face was answer enough for Kamehaloha. Tamara, on the other hand, was much more willing to accept the thread of truth derived from such blatant superstition. And while the fabric of such a tale looked a little foolish when modeled by Kamehaloha, Julian found it all the more charming when worn by the girl.

"Look! A pair of Humpbacks!" Tamara called out from the deck. She pointed to a place not more than a hundred yards off the starboard bow. Kamehaloha followed her line of vision and sighted the whales, also.

"Cut the engines and come down here!" Kong called to Julian, and the novice captain immediately did as he was told. "Have you ever seen anything so beautiful?" he said reverently.

42

"Every time I get close to them it brings tears to my eyes," said Tamara.

Julian stood wide-eyed and excited as he looked out to sea. Searching the horizon, he fervently hoped for a glimpse of the whales.

Kamehaloha searched the waterline through a pair of binoculars. He put his heavy arm around Julian's shoulder, handed him the glasses, and tried to define the area of ocean where he thought the two whales might surface next. "Look for the spray from their blowholes," he advised. "It'll look like a little puff of smoke coming off the water."

Julian put the binoculars to his eyes. At first he saw nothing accept the white crests of the waves. Since the engines had been shut down the boat was rocking with the pitch of the sea, and it was difficult to keep his vision focused upon one area of water. Then he saw the spray; and a moment later the whales breached side by side, two enormous tales following great black forms with white underbellies over the waves and back into the deep. Thrilled by the spectacle, he turned to hand the binoculars to Tamara. "Did you see that?" he exclaimed.

Seconds later the pair surfaced again, this time frolicking on their sides, pectoral fins slapping at the swells.

"They have a language all their own," Kamehaloha explained. "I've heard it, myself! If you place underwater microphones about thirty feet deep, then amplify the sounds, you hear the curious cries and squeaks - in a sequence or a pattern, like code - and it becomes obvious that these are not simply random noises. They have meaning beyond our understanding."

"I think they like us," commented Tamara.

"They're very curious creatures," Kamehaloha said. "If we leave the engines off and just float here awhile, perhaps they'll come even closer!"

But the pair of Humpback whales did not approach the Scoundrel, rather they moved further and further out to sea.

"Maybe we should follow them," Julian suggested.

"Not a good idea," said Kamehaloha. "Like any wild animal, they need their space; and besides, environmental laws against encroachment are very strict." He began moving toward the prow of the boat. "It's getting late," he said. "We should head for Hilo or we'll miss the arrival of *Hawai'iloa*."

He tried to re-start the twin inboards, but once again they seemed to need adjustment. Without concern Kamehaloha made the minor modifications. Julian peered over his shoulder. Meanwhile, Tamara climbed up to the head and stood at the wheel, ready to pilot the cruiser the rest of the way down the Hamakua coast to Hilo. It took the Hawaiian only a few seconds to work his mechanical magic.

On the pier at Hilo Harbor the three friends waited in a jubilant crowd for the triumphal arrival of *Hawai'iloa*. Nainoa Nainoa's six thousand-mile journey was nearly complete.

"This is a great day for Hawaiian people," said Kamehaloha. Pride shone on his round face and in his bright, black eyes.

At the far end of the pier rhythms were being played on traditional drums, and both male and female dancers whirled and undulated in renditions of the sacred *hula*. Slack-key guitars and tinkling ukuleles accompanied ancestral songs sung by burly, ring-shaped men with lilting, falsetto voices. Their attenuated diphthongs and breathy consonants defined a language which sounded simple and sweet.

*Hawai'iloa* came at last into Hilo Harbor, and as the crew struck its sails a cheer went up from the crowd on the dock. Friends exchanged flower *leis*, and colorful *kahili* feathers attached to helium balloons were released into the sky, marking the joyful spirit shared by all. There was a *luau* planned for this afternoon, and everyone was invited, local and *haole* alike.

Leaving the Scoundrel docked in the harbor, the three new friends moved along with the crowd up Banyan Drive. Coming from radically different backgrounds, they seemed quite comfortable together. They joked and laughed at the sight of Kamehaloha - always so carefree and casual - clutching the attaché case filled with money.

44

At Coconut Island Picnic Ground the *luau* was already beginning. There they met a lean and smiley beach boy dressed in shorts and a sloppy T-shirt. With blue eyes and sun-bleached, blond hair, a deep, tropical tan, and a mature blue and yellow macaw parrot riding on top of his left shoulder, the ebullient surfer was at once friendly and familiar, and sidled up close to Tamara.

"Woody Emory! It's been forever!" Tamara beamed. "Let me think... Not since the surfing championships at Pu'ukipu Beach. Where have you been hanging out?"

"I moved to the Big Island about a year ago," he said. "I've been living in Kailua Kona, but I gave up my house last week."

"Why?" she wanted to know.

"I'm heading back to the Mainland," he said.

"But it's so beautiful here," said Julian. "Why would anyone want to leave?"

Woody's smile went on and on as he explained, "I've been living in Hawaii - first on Maui and then on the Big Island - ever since I finished college at Cal Poly. No way was I ready to settle down and get serious right away. And I figured surfing was a more noble occupation anyway - at least for the short term. But now I'm running out of money. It's not the first time for that," he laughed, "but this time I think the cosmos is trying to tell me something."

"Where will you be going?" Tamara wanted to know.

"Silicon Valley," he said. "High tech America awaits!"

"You're not serious, brother," said Kamehaloha.

"I'm afraid so," said Woody. "As a matter of fact, I'm flying to San Francisco tomorrow. The only thing left for me to do is find a good home for Buenaventura," Woody lamented. "I can't take him with me - some idiotic restriction by USDA."

"You mean the bird?" said Julian.

"Right. He's nine years old. I've had him eight years. But I'm afraid we have to part company. It's really a shame. He's a special friend."

"Maybe I could take him," Julian offered.

45

"What do you think, BV?" Woody addressed the bird.

"I'll take excellent care of him," Julian promised. "You'll have to give me a few instructions. Tell me what he likes to eat and drink. All the particulars. But he'll have a good home."

"You live over on Maui?" Woody inquired.

"I've been staying at a friend's condo in Lahaina," he told the surfer, "but I just bought Kamehaloha's cruiser, so I guess I'll be living on the boat from now on."

"So you bought the Scoundrel," said Woody. "What do you know about that?" He looked inconclusively at Kamehaloha. Then at Tamara Sly. Then back at Julian. "Well, Buenaventura won't fly off. At least I don't think he will."

"Does he talk?" Julian asked.

Woody laughed as he stroked the bird's colorful comb. "I'll say he talks! But not always on cue. Sometimes he says the strangest things. He's quite an original thinker, Julian. But I guess you'll just have to see for yourself."

In late afternoon, with the parrot, Buenaventura, now riding on Julian's shoulder, they made their way across the park to the circular barbecue pit where a whole, young *kalua* pig was about to be unearthed. Roasting over smoldering coals and steaming lava rock, the succulent pig had baked the entire day, and as the two young chefs, each naked to the waist and attired below in flower-print sarongs, began to unwrap the multiple layers of ti leaves, the pig's head came off into the ashes. A bevy of onlookers surrounding the pit drew a startled breath at the sight, then laughed, as the two cooks lifted the roasted carcass in a sling. The celebrants applauded the feast they were about to eat.

Served with the roasted pork were several traditional Hawaiian dishes. There was *Lomi* salmon pate, sweet bread, *poi* spread, coconut pudding, mahi mahi or grilled ono fish, wild rice, and plenty of rum drinks. As they feasted, darkness fell. Julian and Kamehaloha became absorbed in the pageantry of a torch-lit, theatrical re-enactment of the *original* Polynesian landing on the Hawaiian Islands.

46

Tamara Sly, conversely, seemed totally engrossed in her long lost friend, Woody Emory. Privately embarrassed, Julian felt disappointed at this turn of events. And when Tamara awkwardly emerged from an all-too-obvious intimacy and announced, "Woody and I are going for a walk down by the lava tube with the fern grotto at its entrance - so don't wait up for me, Julian - I'll meet you back at the Scoundrel...later," well, that took the proverbial wind out of his sails.

That night Julian slept on the deck of the Scoundrel, as did Kamehaloha. When morning came it was obvious that Tamara had not returned. Julian expressed his concern, but Kamehaloha shrugged off her absence. "She's with Woody," he yawned. "No big deal."

"Right," said Julian.

"No big deal," repeated Buenaventura, the first words he'd uttered since his adoption.

"I gotta get a taxi to Hilo Airport," said Kamehaloha. "You think you can handle the Scoundrel?"

"I think so," said Julian, though he was still not totally confident.

"You'll be okay," Kamehaloha reassured. "Just remember how I showed you to adjust those carburetors. And make sure you always have spare gas and extra food. I wouldn't want to read in the paper about some *haole* sailor stranded at sea. Not that I care about you, Julian," he joked, "but the Scoundrel deserves a better fate!"

Julian smiled. "Look, Kamehaloha," he said, "thanks for selling me the Scoundrel. And thanks for the scuba lesson, too. Unlikely as it may seem, I think you've made a difference in my life."

"Hey, brother, maybe I'll see you back on Maui."

They shook hands, then embraced, as the Hawaiian took up his valise full of money and stepped onto the pier.

Chapter 6.

Looking forlorn and a little displaced, BV watched as his new keeper constructed him a permanent living arrangement aboard ship.

"I wonder what happened to Tamara," Julian commented as he finished tying the bird's tether.

"Tomorrow's lie!" croaked BV.

Awash in morning sunlight, Julian sat on deck dressed down to his swimming suit. With pencil and paper in hand he began making a shopping list. If he meant to live on board the Scoundrel with Buenaventura, there were several articles he was going to need: 1) Several containers for storing fresh drinking water; 2) Dry goods like cereal, nuts, pasta, crackers, and canned foods; 3) Seeds and dried fruits for the parrot.

"How do you like your new perch, BV?" Julian asked his new companion.

"Where's Woody?" the parrot wanted to know. "Surf's up!"

"Woody's headed for oblivion in California," Julian observed. "I guess it's just you and me now."

He turned to admire the macaw's striking plumage: blue on the back and wings; yellow on the cockscomb, breast, and tail feathers. Without pandering further comment from the sagacious parrot, Julian assessed the startling intelligence which gleamed in the bird's mocking glance. But surely Buenaventura could not really understand what he was saying...

Julian had decided, also, to outfit the boat with fishing supplies; including rods, nets, lures, tackle, knives, and two or three buckets. He thought a first aid kit was a good idea, too, as well as a basic tool kit. A large tarpaulin might come in handy, and he wanted a woolen navy blanket for damp nights. He would also need cookware and kitchen utensils, as well as extra rope, a winch and pulley, a flashlight, and a hatchet.

"Don't bite through the string and fly away," Julian begged the parrot. "And if Tamara returns while I'm in town, tell her we sail for Maui at three o'clock!"

"Oblivion in California," croaked Buenaventura. He cackled at the top of his voice and rocked from side to side on his new perch. Bobbing his head up and down, he inquired, "Will that be Visa or Mastercard?"

At Yakomoto's General Store Julian bought all the items on his list, as well as several others: including, twenty-five feet of chain; some nails and screws; half a dozen emergency flares; a folder full of nautical maps; and a full set of mechanic's wrenches. When he returned to the wharf, BV was sitting upon his perch underneath the ship's head, one eye closed and his head tucked underneath his wing. Hearing Julian step on board he ruffled up his feathers and cocked his head.

"Tamara Sly!" the bird screamed. "We sail at three!"

"Maybe not," said Julian. "If she doesn't show up soon, we'll be here overnight. I can't imagine anything's happened to her."

"Where's Woody? Surf's up!"

"Apparently, they're old friends," said Julian of Tamara Sly and Woody Emory. "I guess they believe in extended good-byes."

As evening came and the golden sun fell behind towering Mauna Kea, Tamara Sly still had not returned, so Julian resolved to remain docked at Hilo Harbor. If she were not back by

49

morning he would sail without her, and Tamara would have to find her own way back to Maui.

Upon his two-burner propane stove he cooked himself a supper of Campbell's vegetable soup and Rice-a-roni. He drank fresh pineapple juice and ate a chocolate-covered doughnut for dessert. He examined the tools bought at Yokomoto's and arranged them to his liking in the cabinets underneath the head. He put out his toiletry articles - comb, toothbrush, razor, and soap - near the tiny sink, then loaded his new flashlight with fresh batteries. On the pier he busied himself mixing forty-five gallons of extra gasoline with thirty weight oil for the two-cycle engines, then stored it in three separate fifteen-gallon containers - not that he figured to run low between ports, but it was a safety precaution.

Sleeping on his narrow cot Julian dreamed continuously of heavy-featured, dark-skinned Polynesians gyrating in ritual dance. He envisioned fern-draped rain forests resplendent with orchids, hibiscus, and plumeria. Brightly colored tropical birds - Buenaventura's avis friends and relatives - were all chatting one another up! At dawn he awoke refreshed and happy.

For breakfast he ate granola, strawberries, and condensed milk, carefully separating all the almonds, walnuts, and cashews, to feed the bird. Later he organized his fishing gear, periodically looking up and down the pier for any sign of Tamara.

By eleven o'clock it was obvious she was not going to show up. Perhaps she'd bought a ticket at the last minute and taken the flight to San Francisco with Woody Emory.

At noon he guided the Scoundrel out of Hilo Harbor and headed south along the coastline of the Big Island. Julian had no trouble whatsoever handling the large cruiser, and the ship performed without flaw. The powerful inboards took him out of Hilo Bay and around Pohoiki Point, past Kalapana and the lava flows at the Chain of Craters. By two-thirty he reached South Point. With the warm sunshine on his face, and Buenaventura riding on top of his shoulder, Julian steered his ship.

Mid-afternoon was hot along the densely treed cliffs of the Kona coast. The swells broke along the barrier reef, and the blue waters of the Pacific awakened in Julian some distant remembrance of integral color - deep, transfixing impressions of azure and violet - inviting, cool and rejuvenating. The tropical sun had turned his skin cinnamon brown. He wished for a friendly shower, that he might feel clean in some new and intimate way. But today his wish was in vain. So he drew a long breath of the forest's newly made oxygen. Then he forgot himself.

He dropped anchor in Kealakekua Bay just after four o'clock and stared out at the same crescent-shaped coastline which Captain Cook had seen two hundred years before. But unlike Cook's arrival, there were no double-hulled canoes carrying the *Alii* rowing out to meet him; there were no bare-breasted, Polynesian nymphs swimming playfully round his ship, ready and willing to climb on board and bestow their own special kind of *aloha*.

Buenaventura offered his own spurious observation: "Captain Cook... What a crook!"

Aboard the Scoundrel Julian was at home wherever he found himself at day's end. After eating supper he watched the radiant colors of a glorious sunset. At dusk the stars appeared low and bright over the calm waters of Kealakekua Bay, and few onshore lights glared against the depths of infinity. Julian felt at once diminutive and boundless. Sitting on deck he devoted himself to the practice of tying and untying knots.

North of the Big Island, with the south coast of Maui already in sight, the Scoundrel's engines began coughing like a smoker after too many Pall Malls. Finally each, in turn, belched a last gasp of blue smoke and sputtered pathetically into silence. Julian went immediately for his tool kit and tried to adjust the carburetors just as Kamehaloha had shown him. After a full hour of diligent tinkering he could not make the engines turn over, and the Scoundrel was cast adrift in the calm waters of the Hawaiian archipelago.

The straight between the Big Island and Maui was well traveled, and surely someone would come along sooner or later to offer assistance. Julian was not feeling upset at Kamehaloha over

51

the Scoundrel's breakdown, rather he was perturbed by his own mechanical ineptitude.

"A fine mess you've gotten us into this time," taunted Buenaventura.

"I'm sorry," said Julian. "I tried to adjust the engines, but it's not working. Maybe *you* have a suggestion."

"I wouldn't be making any plans," the parrot croaked.

"Thanks for the encouragement," said the captain.

Julian hoisted his distress flag and determined to wait. About an hour after they were stranded a boat full of camera-carrying tourists pulled up alongside the Scoundrel. "What seems to be the trouble?" called the tour guide from the head of his boat.

"Both my engines are down," said Julian.

"How long have you been out here?"

"Not long. Only an hour or so."

"Do you want a lift back to Kailua?" he offered.

"Actually, I'd rather not leave my boat," said Julian. "But I'd appreciate it if you'd contact a two-cycle mechanic and have him come out to give me a little help."

"Do you have water and food?" the tour guide asked.

"Plenty of each," Julian confirmed.

"What's the name of your boat?"

"The Scoundrel," said Julian.

The guide looked at him rather queerly. "Are you sure you want to wait? It might take quite a while for help to arrive," he warned.

"I'll be fine," said Julian.

"Then drop your anchor and sit tight," said the tour captain. "Try not to move off your position until somebody gets here."

"Right. Well, it looks like I'm *not* going anywhere," said Julian.

"That's what you think," intoned Buenaventura.

Julian was truly disappointed that Tamara Sly had not returned in time to sail with the Scoundrel - that he had not waited a little longer for her. Were they to be stranded together off the Kona coast, a serendipitous opportunity for intimacy might have been theirs.  Not that he needed such a contrived situation to charm a woman.  Or did he?  In truth, he'd not dated anyone since the break-up of his marriage.

Julian moved to the one mirror on board the Scoundrel and began examining his own face.  He was momentarily struck with the curious impression of some former self.  He looked relaxed.  Sun-colored, high cheekbones seemed to brighten his aspect.  His brows were light and sandy, as were newly grown whiskers.  His earlobes and the tops of his shoulders were crimson from time spent in the tropical sun, and fine skin flaked off his forehead after initial sunburn.  Still, he very much liked the rich coloring he'd acquired in Hawaii, for he'd not had a decent tan in years.

As the sun went down help still had not arrived, and Julian concluded that he and BV would spend the night adrift.  In the distance Mauna Kea was cast in dramatic silhouette against the cloudless golden sky, and the tranquil waters off the Kona coast also gleamed in the aureate twilight.  He cooked pork and beans on his propane stove.  He ate a mango, drank some sangria.  He put out a variety of seeds and dried fruits for Buenaventura.  Together they watched the stars come out, and the ocean rocked the cruiser gently, as if it were a newborn's cradle.

"Why do we lose touch with the wonders of nature?" Julian asked rhetorically.

"Speak for yourself, cowboy," advised Buenaventura.

Julian laughed as he swallowed some of the sweetened wine.  He ate one of BV's sunflower seeds and said, "I suppose it's very different in *your* world - the animal world."

His familiar did not speak, but seemed to nod in acknowledgment.

Now in full darkness Julian lay on his bunk thinking:

'Longest night of year,
Or deepest night of soul,
Perhaps one's vestigial longings
Always make it so...'

\* \* \* \* \*

Eleven years ago, as a family of three, they had celebrated his daughter's twelfth birthday with an outing to Sea World. After touring the complex they'd rode the trolley to San Diego's Gas Lamp Quarter to shop for Kirsten's birthday present. Julian no longer remembered what she'd chosen but he did recall a disagreement between Kirsten and Kelly, his ex-wife. His daughter had displayed one of her distinctive tantrums, while Kelly turned a stoic cheek. Once the fight was settled they eased the friction by strolling the tree-lined boulevards and pathways in Balboa Park, eating ice cream cones and watching buskers perform in the outdoor amphitheater.

Over the next seven years marital intimacy and familial cohesion had deteriorated silently and steadily, and in the end Julian and Kelly had come to the mutual conclusion that progressive diminution was far worse than separation. The eventual divorce was anticlimactic.

Having bought their Torrey Pines house when California real estate was a terrific bargain, the sale of the property left them both financially comfortable. Kelly and Kirsten moved to LA. Kirsten, (nearly an adult herself), remained dispassionate regarding her parents' divorce, and floundered for a time trying to find herself. Eventually she moved to Seattle. Julian rented a condo in downtown San Diego.

Then, at age fifty-two, the 'option' of early retirement was presented to Julian and others by his company's Board of Directors. The offer was not an ultimatum, but Crosby was no fool. Down-sizing was a mark of the times, as well as a poignant reality in his own life! The severance package put on the table was overly generous, and given a set of uncertain alternatives Julian was not disinclined to being bought out.

Here on his boat, amidst a tangle of ropes and hooks, he recapped the rather hideous highlights of a luncheon held in his honor the day of his so-called retirement.

After several rounds of drinks and a catered meal, his fellow employees had presented him with the rather extravagant gift of a Rolex watch. Each co-worker offered congratulations,

54

their own professional insecurities obvious in their barbs. Julian didn't know whether to laugh or cry.

"You're a lucky dog," said Denny Jackson as he handed him the watch. "Now you have all the time in the world!"

"Easy for you to say," Julian returned good-naturedly. "You still have your job."

"Look, Crosby, next year it'll probably be one of us. And they won't be offering us the sweet package they gave you!"

Julian remembered telephoning Kevin Miles once he'd left the luncheon.

"Taking the afternoon off?" asked the broker.

"I may be taking the rest of my life off," said Julian drolly. "The guys at Palisades gave me a retirement party this afternoon."

"I didn't know you were retiring early," Miles said.

"That makes two of us."

"So you're not entirely happy about it?"

"I really don't know how I feel yet, Kevin."

"A pat on the back and a boot in the ass, eh?"

"And a pretty sizable check, too," said Julian.

"These days it's SOP, my friend."

"I know. But it doesn't make it any easier."

"At least money's not a worry," Kevin consoled.

"I guess time is the real enemy," Julian stammered.

"That's the truth," Miles agreed.

"I'm too young to be cast away."

"Of course you are, Julian. But perhaps you have to embrace this as an opportunity! Tell me something you've always wanted to do," said Miles. "Something you never imagined you'd have the guts to follow up!"

"How would I know?" said Julian. "Choice is a rather novel idea in my life."

"I'm serious," his friend persisted. "What's the first thing that comes to your mind?"

"I suppose I always wanted to buy a boat," Julian confessed.

Julian could hear that Miles was preoccupied with another task as they spoke, and the lack of singular attention was irritating. "You never seemed much like the boat type to me," said the broker. "But who am I to question your dreams? You've got the money."

"I could buy a houseboat or a cabin cruiser and dock it at Sausalito Harbor. After all, why should I tether myself to this place?"

"Or you could head over to Hawaii," Kevin suggested. "Have you ever been there?"

"No, I haven't," said Julian.

"Ten years ago I got a great deal on a condo. I've been over there dozens of times, and I'm telling you, Julian, you'll come back a new man - that is, if you come back at all!"

How odd that an off-the-cuff conversation had turned into reality, detail by detail. Though Julian Crosby was certainly harboring no regrets. On the contrary, he felt grateful to Miles for rekindling his fantasy. And as the first fiery rays of morning light engaged the new day, Julian rose slowly from recapitulation and assessment to discover his anchor was gone.

All reference points now receding, and balance and dimension in serious question, Julian kept track of the days and wondered just how the Scoundrel had been set adrift. He saw not a single ship on the horizon, though he thought he might have heard the hopeful sound of an airplane's motor, circling. He continued searching the sky for fifteen minutes after the sound faded. Nothing. Except a solitary Calico Pennant dragonfly. If he thought he'd known loneliness before, the overwhelming magnitude of abandonment now settled over him like a vacuum.

"Captain Crosby, I've learned that a threat of mutiny is circulating among the crew," revealed Buenaventura.

"But you *are* the crew," said Julian.

The bird turned a somersault on his perch. He ruffled his feathers, winked at Julian, and began chattering riddles. "This is *Electra* calling *Itasca*. We are running on line. Will repeat. Will repeat..."

"What are you talking about?" Julian wanted to know.

"Merciless life laughs in the burning sun..."

"I don't get it!" Julian protested.

"No trailing wire antenna. No Morse code key," the parrot mocked, shaking his yellow head. "No parachute, either. Just a pilot's swan song. Like looking for a pimple on the backside of an elephant. Nothing but ocean."

Indeed...

By night the fragmented images of dreams danced round the borders of Julian's prescience, but with each morning, prospect and promise faded in the dizzying gray circumference, and hope turned into parcels of doubt regarding his rescue. Though not once did he feel fear. Each hour spent in this whirlpool of dismissal seemed to promote a curiously heightened sense of self-awareness. Anticipation engaged him on a more subliminal tangent.

How many days had it been? Eighteen, he thought. Though by now his count may have been way off. His blond beard grew full and bristly; his lips turned purple, swollen, and cracked. He heard only the rolling swells day and night, and the circling plane as it made its once-a-day incursion.

Many futile attempts to re-start the Scoundrel's engines caused Julian to renounce all trust in the rationality of the mechanical world. Yet even had he been able to coax the motors back to life, on which heading would he have sailed? All sense of direction had been lost by his third day adrift. Now he floated without reference upon the unfathomable Face of the Deep.

Night came again and the castaway lay upon his cot. He moved without restraint from cabin into cosmos and back again. He dreamed of himself as a much younger man in a state more virile than he'd ever truthfully known. Hurled over waves and plunged into aquatic troughs, he had an ejaculation, and awoke feeling incomplete.

With the drone of dimensional drift resounding hypnotically in his ears, (Or was this merely the habitual appearance of the spectral phoenix circling overhead, once more on the margin of emanation?), Julian got to his feet and climbed

57

the ladder to the head. The morning sky was gray and threatening and the sea was rough. Tossed over rolling walls of foamy water, then flung over breakers with the finality of castigating judgment, the Scoundrel survived as thunderous curls crashed against prow. The foundling held on for dear life as the parrot flapped his wings frantically and tried to free himself from his tether.

"All is lost! Abandon ship, Captain!" screamed Buenaventura.

"Hold on tight!" Julian called.

"We're out of time!" proclaimed the parrot.

As the curtain of fog parted before him, Julian could distinguish beaches ringed by palm trees and lush mountains crowned by low clouds. An island lay directly ahead. And a tumultuous tide hurled the Scoundrel toward a protected cove.

Just then the bird broke free from his tether and took wing. Cutting through a stiff wind BV flew with conviction for the perceived safety of the rain forest, and Julian called after him desperately, "Wait! Wait!"

But the macaw was lost.

The novice sailor tried valiantly to steer his craft to a gentle landing, but, whirling and pitching, the Scoundrel defied guidance. Finally thrown from the head to the deck, Julian clung to a railing, barely avoiding being tossed overboard.

Moments later the ship ran aground on top of the barrier reef. Julian climbed to his feet and stared out in astonishment at the island's sandy shoreline only a hundred yards away. He sighed gratefully. A vigorous swim reunited him with dry land.

Chapter 7.

It was not yet dawn but a crowd of curiosity seekers and well-wishers gathered in the dim light on the tarmac at Miami. Each onlooker was hoping to catch a glimpse of Miss Amelia Earhart dressed in flying togs and silk scarf as she climbed on board her *Electra* for take-off.

Publicity for this around-the-world flight attempt was, thanks to G.P., quite intense, and a company of journalists, along with a newsreel film crew, stood by as several mechanics made last minute inspections. Available earlier for reporters and photographers, the pilot and her husband had retreated to the privacy of an empty airplane hangar to express their farewells.

Together they sat on a cold concrete step. The plumbless surroundings were familiar; the circumstances inescapable. Her eyes were calm and clear. He was transparently anxious. She placed her delicate hands in his much larger ones as she spoke in a low voice.

"I know that if I fail, or if I'm lost, you'll be blamed. Our backers will second guess you for allowing me to leave on this trip. But this is my responsibility - mine alone!"

"I'll call or cable at every opportunity," he promised.

When the chief mechanic gave the 'all-ready' she stood up, pressed her husband's hands again, took a deep breath, then walked from the cavernous hangar. Freddy was waiting next to the *Electra*. Together they boarded the plane. They waved to reporters and photographers, to relatives and spectators.

The prep crew backed away as she throttled up the engines. The running lights were flashing as G.P. lowered his head to say a short prayer. Inside the cockpit Amelia made a final check of her instruments, adjusted her goggles, then gave a 'thumbs up'.

Weighted with fuel the *Electra* lumbered down the long runway. The crowd held its breath until the plane finally rose in the haze of daybreak. As the plane slowly climbed, the sun appeared above the aquatic horizon. Everyone watched until the *Electra* was out of sight. Then the crowd dispersed - all except George Palmer Putnam. He remained on the tarmac long after everyone else had gone inside.

Their first destination was San Juan, Puerto Rico, a route which Freddy had plotted many times while navigating for Pan Am. Averaging one hundred forty-eight miles per hour, they covered the distance in just over seven hours, and Noonan's flawless calculations estimated landfall within one minute of actual touchdown.

From Puerto Rico they flew from Caripito, Venezuela; then on to Paramaribo, Dutch Guiana. Forteleza, a regional commercial center located along the northeast coast of Brazil, boasted Ceara's largest airport and best maintenance facility. The distance between Forteleza and Natal, Brazil's easternmost point, Amelia covered with the aid of the Sperry autopilot.

The flight from Natal to Dakar, Senegal crossed the Atlantic at its shortest distance. The nineteen hundred mile flight was, for the most part, uneventful, though Amelia began to smell gas fumes shortly after take-off. Unable to identify the source of the leak, she determined to have the maintenance crew at Dakar identify the problem.

Thirteen hours into the flight they approached Cape Verde Peninsula, Africa's westernmost point. On the notorious fishing line installed for communication between pilot and navigator, Freddy passed forward a note describing a minor course correction: 'Change to 36 degrees. Estimate 79 miles to Dakar from 3:36 p.m.'

Amelia immediately scribbled and inquiry: 'What put us north?'

Not trusting Noonan's fix she banked north, not south as instructed. Following the African shoreline she ended up fifty miles off course, at Saint Louis, Senegal. Forced to admit her mistake, she openly apologized to Freddy. Next morning they flew to Dakar for a layover. While the *Electra* was undergoing thorough scrutiny, they toured Cheikh Anta Diop University and rested up from their transatlantic crossing. They mailed home no-longer-needed South American maps and documents.

Over equatorial Africa, en route to Khartoum, Fred Noonan found navigation to be even more difficult than over open sea. Between Fort Lamy and El Fashar the so-called landmarks were often seasonal or ambiguous: 'swamp during rain', or, 'two helig trees four hundred meters apart - intersecting twenty-fourth meridian.' But as the navigator struggled in stifling heat with mathematics and direction-finding, the quixotic pilot openly delighted at flying over places once relegated to a position only in fantasy - places such as: Qala-en Hahl; Umm Shinayshin; Abu Seid; Idd el Bashir; Fazi; Marabia Abu Fas...

From Massawa they continued down the Red Sea coast to the ancient port of Assab in Italian-controlled Eritrea. Here the temperature approached one hundred degrees, and they flew at low altitude over groups of nomad shepherds who pointed skyward with great excitement at the *Electra*. Amelia conjectured that it was possible many of these Tigre people had never before seen an airplane.

Expressly forbidden to land on Arab soil, the pilot flew around the Arabian Peninsula, then northwest of the Indus River delta, all the way to Karachi. There she talked with G.P. by telephone.

"I wish you were here," she told him. "So many things you would enjoy... Perhaps someday we can fly together to some of the remote places of the world - just for fun!"

At Calcutta the air field was sodden. With even more monsoon rain in the forecast, they decided to refuel and take off immediately for Burma. The plane clung to the sticky soil of the runway for what seemed like ages before the wheels finally lifted. They cleared the fringe of trees at the aerodrome's edge with only inches to spare.

Now en route for eighteen days, they turned inland from the Gulf of Martaban and flew twenty-five miles over saturated rice paddies to the city of Rangoon. After a formal State reception they were taken by proud and friendly Burmese officials to visit the Shwe Dagon Pagoda, the core of Burmese religious life. They learned about Alaungpaya, founder of the final royal dynasty in Burma, and about the history of Dagon/Rangoon, whose name, they were told, translated roughly to mean, 'the end of strife.'

By now the rigors of travel coupled with the enforced manners of cultural exchange had begun to take its toll. Patience between pilot and navigator had been well tested, but even as feelings between them began to turn ambivalent, such experiences were not lightly shared.

In Bangkok, (the city of angels), they rode elephants and toured the exotic canal-lined streets with characteristic houses perched upon stilts. They walked through the street markets and visited the extraordinary walled Grand Palace to see the Wat Po and the Wat Emerald Buddha.

Hemmed in by volcanic peaks covered with vegetation, Bandung, on the Island of Java, was refreshing with its cool, wet, upland climate. Here their take-off was delayed by bad weather, though neither Amelia nor Fred was particularly upset. They were tired and needed rest. Furthermore, three of the *Electra's* long distance instruments had been malfunctioning. The fuel analyzer, the flow meter, and generator meter would be crucial for the upcoming over-water flights. So the equipment was repaired while they waited for a break in the monsoon.

They finally took off from Bandung on the 27th of June. Stopping in nearby Jakarta, they indulged themselves in a dinner of *rijsttafel*, a traditional Indonesian feast consisting of rice with no less than twenty-one courses of fish, chicken, meats, eggs, relishes, curries, nuts, fruits, vegetables, and sauces. Unfortunately, a hit-and-run bout with dysentery followed. Already fatigued, the illness further compromised Amelia's faltering endurance.

En route to Port Darwin, Australia, the pilot again noticed the unmistakable smell of gasoline - a specious rupture whose source had so far not been identified even during several all-out overhauls. Confined and virtually immobile for long periods of time in the cockpit, the pervasive vapors made her feel ill as she flew. Mechanics in Port Darwin meticulously inspected the plane point by point, but ultimately found no breach in the fuel system.

The relentless pace of travel dictated by State clearances was proving deleterious. In less than a month they'd circumnavigated two thirds of the globe, stopping infrequently for rest. At each layover numerous details demanded attention. Customs inspections and forms, fumigation of the *Electra*, inoculation certificates, obtaining accurate weather reports for the next segment of the trip, supervising chamois filtration of the fuel.

The night before the Howland flight Amelia slept very little. Instead, she spent hours writing detailed articles for publication in the *International Herald Tribune*. Freddy was occupied socializing at the Cecil Hotel's bar with Eric Chaters, head administrator at Lea Airport.

"As a navigator, your reputation is unquestioned, Freddy," bolstered Chaters. "But being able to pinpoint Howland Island is going to be your ultimate test. I'm glad I won't be sitting in your seat..."

While his companion was nursing a beer, Freddy Noonan had already slugged down several shots of straight whiskey. "Don't worry, Eric," he reassured. "I'll have no trouble finding the island..."

63

At Lea, the *Electra* was serviced yet again. Oil and oil filters were changed, spark plugs were cleaned, engines checked and re-checked. The fluctuating fuel pump and Sperry autogiro were again performing erratically, so they were taken apart and repaired for the third time. Luckily, the Lea maintenance crew was thoroughly familiar with Lockheed aircraft, and both Amelia and Freddy were duly impressed by their expertise and ability.

With the *Electra* left in capable hands, the pilot and navigator spent their last hours in Asia boxing up unwanted articles to be shipped home, items that included the Very flare pistol and its cartridges, and the two parachutes. In case of emergency these would be of little use over water.

At last they were ready for take-off from Lea, New Guinea. Ahead lay miles of boundless ocean, an obscure island, midway to Hawaii, where Roosevelt's DOC had constructed a landing strip specifically for this trip, and finally, San Francisco.

At ten o'clock a.m., loaded with more than a thousand gallons of fuel, the *Electra* moved over Lea's unpaved runway without so much as a breeze to help lift the overburdened plane into the air. The craft gained speed as it hurtled toward the seaward end of the runway, and as the wheels hit the crest of the runway's tip, the plane virtually bounced into the air. At first unable to gain altitude due to the heavy load, the *Electra* hovered only a few feet above the swells, its props spraying sea water onto the windshield of the cockpit. Coaxed by the capable pilot, it finally began to climb. Slowly it rose to a hundred feet. Then five hundred. As it disappeared from view, Amelia's Lockheed was still no more than a thousand feet above the ocean.

Right from the beginning head winds were stronger than forecasted, and fuel consumption was proportionately greater than expected. Yet, with the crescent-shaped coast of New Britain on her left, and Bougainvillea Island just ahead, the pilot was glad to finally embark upon this long-anticipated flight over Oceana. She knew the dangers, but they'd planned well. And if she'd ever doubted her navigator's ability, she was now thoroughly convinced of his skill. For even across North Africa, where landmarks were few, and gaining a sense of direction seemed all but impossible, Freddy's readings had been flawless. Throughout the trip he'd kept them precisely on course and delivered them to each destination virtually within minutes of his projection.

Yet she knew that navigating the Pacific posed unique problems. And there remained the intriguing side bar of President Roosevelt's clandestine picture-taking detour - a service both she and Fred agreed they were willing to render.

But as she radioed her position over Nukumanu, Amelia realized she was already running a full hour behind her flight plan. Only a third of the way to Howland, she understood there was virtually no way of making up the lost time, thereby compromising range due to increased fuel consumption. To make matters more difficult, the clouds had grown thick as they flew northeast. Noonan passed her a note on the inter-cabin fishing line that read: 'Six hours on dead reckoning. Need celestial fix. Can you climb on top?'

Amelia powered up the engines with a rich fuel mixture, and the *Electra* responded immediately. Up they rose above cruising altitude. Trying to break through the dense ceiling, the wings began to ice over; and the pilot was forced to descend without gaining the navigator's needed reading. Shortly, she found a break in the clouds and tried again. This attempt consumed even more fuel than the first try, however the effort proved worthwhile. The navigator was able to establish position. Now a crucial question demanded an answer: Should they turn north toward Truk Island in the Carolines, or should they abort their ancillary mission because of adverse flying conditions?

'How's the fuel consumption curve?' Freddy wanted to know.

Amelia scribbled a note and reeled it back into Freddy's compartment amidst the auxiliary fuel tanks. 'I think we're O.K. Weather questionable...'

'We go on your judgment,' came the reply.

AE was flattered by Freddy's trust, and a little surprised by his courage. Bottom line, she could not disappoint the president. 'Please describe alternate heading,' she wrote. In a matter of minutes the course adjustment was in her hand.

But immediately after turning north they began to encounter difficult weather. Not wanting to fly directly into rain squalls, the pilot tried to steer the plane around each approaching storm center, flying fifty miles due north of one, thirty miles south of another. Increased wind velocity made the plane precess consistently starboard, rendering the gyroscopic compass and the autopilot quite useless. She calmly searched heavy skies for a 'soft spot' in the storm, but unwittingly flew right into the nucleus of the tempest.

The *Electra* bounced and pitched with a vengeance. Lightning illuminated the churning storm clouds in their flight path, and rain beat against the windshield, nullifying all sense of depth and direction. She fought against the twenty-five degree bank like a cowboy trying to break an obstinate horse.

And like a semaphore flag barely visible in the ultraviolet glow of the instrument panel, a new message appeared from Noonan on the infernal fishing line. She snatched the paper off the clothespin and cursed. Her hands were busy simply trying to keep the plane level; and she was perturbed by the navigator's question: 'Any chance of getting on top?'

It was ten minutes before her hands were free enough to jot a frustrated reply: 'What am I supposed to do?'

His response was unemotional yet to the point. 'My compass shows us seven degrees off course.'

Freddy was correct; they *were* off course. The magnetic compass was swinging so wildly that she was forced to determine a heading by averaging its readings, hoping to make corrections once they cleared the squalls.

And her arm ached from priming the '*wobble*' pump. Her back hurt from the ten-hour-long confinement in the four-foot by four-foot cockpit. She smelled gas again, and the odor made her feel nauseous. Becoming increasingly alarmed by the apparent rate of fuel consumption, she ciphered her own calculations. Despite bucking stiff head winds, it was *not* reconcilable. More fuel should have been in reserve.

66

Another note along the 'line of communication' read: 'Desperate for a reading. When?'

She penciled a reply and fastened it to their peculiar conduit: 'Should I expend fuel for another climb?'

Freddy's frustrated reply left no doubt: 'We're lost!'

Without delay she richened the mixture and throttled up. The *Electra* climbed to ten thousand feet. She switched on the landing lights to determine just how thick the vapor might be. But it was impossible to see anything. So she pulled back on the stick and took the plane to eleven thousand feet. Then twelve thousand. Still nothing. Thirteen thousand. Fourteen. That was *Electra's* absolute ceiling. Where was the top?

She tried to yell above the incessant roar of the engines, though she could barely hear the sound of her own voice. "Damn it, Freddy Noonan! Take your sextant reading now. I can't hold it here forever..."

And she leaned into the stick for the descent. Back into the rain, the plane precessed to port. She corrected. Again it lurched. Calmly, she reacted. Then came the navigator's note: 'No hope for pictures at Truk Island. Must abort. New heading for Marshalls to follow. Majuro Island by sun-up.'

Amelia hooted out loud. She sighed in relief and wiped perspiration from her face. They'd been successful; Freddy had fixed their position. They were probably low on fuel, but at least they weren't lost...

PART II.

Chapter 1.

Again she walked the well-worn path of evocation, through the 'Grove of Many Dragons'. Under the morning's dun sky, subaqueous spirits embraced the energy of the vegetable world, and a hundred thousand tapered points quivered in the breeze of the storm's aftermath. In her hand she carried a stone from the beach, washed smooth by the waves and collected at the mouth of the delta. There the waters of the Seven Sisters moved over the rocks on their way to the sea.

Otherwise featureless, the egg-shaped stone, now wrapped in a yellow tea leaf, would be her offering to Mo'o, the serpentine god she'd never actually seen, (though she'd once felt his cold hand upon her leg). Mo'o lived at the bottom of the pool where the twin waterfalls cascaded over a ninety-foot embankment and plunged into the largest of seven descending pools. From the water she drew her vitality.

As she danced to the rhythms of the tropics, lost in time, the rain forest was her only partner. Inveterate ferns cloaked the forest floor like decorative ruffles along the hem of a full skirt; and were contrasted by the vibrant and prolific red blooms of the Poinciana. The aerial roots of the banyan trees sought the moisture of the volcanic earth, and tall palms opened like

68

umbrellas overhead. The yellow, red, and green ti leaves and arching bamboo shoots filled every open space, and broad-leafed philodendrons wound round and round the gnarled bark of the monkeypods. The twisting trunks of the dracaenas reminded her of her own divergent destiny. Shortly after her arrival on the island - immersed in the largest of the seven pools - she had chosen to re-christen herself. The relinquishing of her outworn persona came after an incisive and perilous twist of fate - a crash landing. Marooned and quite alone in Paradise, it was essential that she befriend herself without qualification, and she bestowed upon herself the immutable and loyal appellation, Amie.

Placing her offering on top of a volcanic stone at pool side, she heard the distant rumble of thunder. Last night's storm was moving away. During her time spent as a castaway, Amie had weathered countless storms, yet this morning she felt uneasy. Something unspecified, and perhaps unwanted, remained in the wake of the tempest.

Tossing her long hair back she unfastened the sennit rope that held her skirt round her waist and let the garment drop to the ground. She took the flower lei from her neck and carefully placed it nearby. Bending down, she noticed a small spider spinning its gossamer web among the ferns. The tiny arachnid's home was an intricate network of connection, as was her own. With eyes raised and arms outstretched she paid homage, as she did each morning, to the spirits of earth, air, fire, and water. Bathed in temporal light she stood naked and unashamed.

Amie moved to the side of the pool, her lengthy stride declaring a propensity to motion. Gazing innocently into the crystalline water she drew a single, amazed breath, for she barely recognized her own reflected image.

Her blue-gray eyes shone clear and lucid, her face tawny and smooth. Spreading over her cheeks, nose, and forehead, a precipitous field of freckles lent her face comic relief. A small gap between her two front teeth, which she'd had since childhood, continued to make her self-conscious about her smile even though there was nobody here to see it. Over time her lips had grown fuller, and the tiny crow's feet around her eyes had mysteriously disappeared. Amie admired her fine neck and proud shoulders and recalled how her long legs and slim hips had once been perfect for Coco Chanel's *nouveau* fashions. The passing years had not diminished her figure in the least. If anything, it was even better now.

Indulging a moment of recapitulation, she tossed a pebble into the pool and watched as concentric circles spread out over the top of the placid water. How many years had passed? There was really no way of knowing how long she'd been marooned on the island. Seasonable variation was quite subtle, and the meridian at which the sun rose and set deviated not more than a couple of degrees. The procession of days came and went without tangible distinction, and weeks turned into months, months into years.

In the beginning the establishment of rituals had helped her maintain her sanity in the face of isolation and loneliness. Over time such routines became a spiritual comfort. Ephemeral symbols evolved and deepened; her daily devotions became more joy than habit.

Shortly after her arrival Amie ventured away from the sandy, palm-lined coast to explore the inland territory. The beach front surrendered suddenly to a razory cluster of peaks. Each one, she estimated, rose to an altitude of greater than a thousand feet. While scrambling up an immense stone platform that lay nearly hidden by the dense overgrowth, she came near the cinder cone - a crater measuring as much as seventy-five yards in diameter. From her narrow foothold she looked down from the summit at the reef that encircled the island.

While the atoll was apparently now untenanted by other humans, certain discoveries led her to suspect past habitation. In a clearing near the mouth of the volcano she came upon what appeared to be an ancient temple. Stone seats surrounded a great altar. Indeed, no artifact could have spoken more eloquently of the island's extinct culture.

Looking southward she observed hardened black lava fields. Parched and faded grasses grew between the cracks and fissures of the brittle pumice. What an awesome display of power and beauty such a cataclysm would have unsealed! Now the volcano lay mottled green across pearly waters.

Wading into the pool and treading water, Amie returned her attention to the present. She cupped her hands and drew cool water over her face. Instantly she felt renewed. The morning's illustrious sunlight reflected off the ripples in the cool water, and Amie swam near a great protruding stone, where she rested on a ledge. Only then did she hear a voice - the first, other than her own, in what seemed an eternity.

"*I only have eyes for you...*" came the song from a source hidden somewhere within the proliferous, overhanging vegetation. Such an unexpected incursion rattled her sensibilities.

The shiny, blue and yellow plumage of a macaw parrot shone through the deep green depths of the tropical rain forest, and with perfect vision Amie segregated the first-time visitor without difficulty. Hardly accustomed to receiving company, Amie laughed aloud, and the macaw, in turn, imitated her laughter. "What are you doing here?" she asked innocently.

"What are *you* doing here?" he echoed.

"I was marooned here a long time ago," she offered. "What about you?"

Through the misty spray of the waterfall Buenaventura perceived the island's only resident in a spectral array of light, and he was first inclined to liken her splendor to that of a rainbow.

"I'm a mutineer," was all he elected to disclose.

"After all this time spent alone, you can't know how wonderful it is to finally hear the sound of another voice," Amie said. "Even if you *are* a parrot!"

Amie climbed out of the water and lay down upon a flat rock to dry herself in the sunshine. With both hands she wrung water from her wavy, riotous hair, then tried to untangle its curly ends. "Why not perch closer so I can have a better look at you?" she suggested to the bird.

Buenaventura ignored her request; rather he responded with a bit of original poetry:

71

"People think I'm timid,
And people think I'm tame,
But that just goes to show,
I'm wilder than you know,
Fate turns on the axis of my name."

"I can't believe what I'm hearing," said Amie, delighted.

"Keep in touch!" baited BV as he spread his wings and flew away.

Amie's world was truly a private place. She barely separated herself from its earthly cadence, though it had not always been so. Walking from the bathing pool downstream toward her home near the beach front, she contemplated the unexpected encounter with the loquacious parrot and was suddenly conscious of how accustomed she'd grown to living alone. Perhaps over time she'd even come to cherish the solitude...

Of course integration had not been easy. In those first uncertain days procuring basic needs superseded all else. Thankfully fresh fruit was obvious and plentiful, though finding adequate shelter was an issue not easily resolved. The very thought of going back to the plane made her shake uncontrollably, so she slept on the warm sand, where the sea front vegetation edged the strand.

At first she dreamed repeatedly of the crash - the initial loss of control, the sensation of time slowing down, and finally the jolt of impact. She'd prepared for a water landing, but in dense fog the plane had grazed the side of an indiscernible mountain. Tumbling end over end, the mangled craft came to rest in a field of ferns. The only passenger, her navigator, had died in the defining moment of his life, and she was barely able to contain her grief and guilt. In the confusion of her own survival the devastated pilot crawled from the ruined aircraft. Looking for help she hobbled, in amazement and denial, through the dense rain forest, but met with only the profound and eerie silence of a deserted Shangri-La. Following the course of a swiftly-running stream she was able to reach the shoreline, where she collapsed in shock.

When she regained consciousness, she bound an open leg wound with the remnants of a torn shirtsleeve. She tried to unsnarl strands of hair matted with dried blood. She washed her face with sea water. The salt stung her eyes. Trying to reconcile her situation she searched sky and horizon for any sign of a rescue party. The Cutter, *Itasca*, must be nearby, she thought. Nothing... Feelings of desperation surfaced, and she tried not to give way. Of course a massive search would be launched once it was determined that they were delinquent at Howland Island. G.P. was a person of action; he knew how to set a plan in motion. And the president would not disavow knowledge of her mission... So she lit a fire on the beach, and kept it burning day and night.

During her third night on the island it began to rain just after dark. The castaway huddled beneath the wide canopy of a spreading monkeypod tree in a futile attempt to stay dry. Next morning, soaked to the skin, she determined to make herself a shelter.

Among the branches of the monkeypod, Amie constructed her house. Making rope ladders from banyan vines for access to the tree's lower branches, she industriously fashioned a wood floor from the fallen limbs of a nearby koa tree. Lashing together two-inch thick branches with braided sennit rope, she planed the wood with an adz fashioned from a piece of sharp coral. And weaving together dried grasses found up-shore with freshly-gathered, spiky palm fronds, she fabricated a thatched, conical roof that she covered with philodendron leaves laid like shingles to shed rain water. In place of solid walls she made large bamboo shades that could be raised by a drawstring in good weather, and lowered when it rained.

Determined to survive, she gradually assembled the elements essential for day-to-day living. And though she dreaded a return to the site of the crash, she gathered courage and made her way back to the plane's wreckage. She knew she could re-fashion parts of the *Electra* into much needed items for this new and imposed lifestyle.

Reaching the crash site she was caught off guard by the devastation. Such chaos poignantly certified the end of erstwhile goals and aspirations, and she wept for connections she might never again engage. So massive was the damage that she was forced to disregard the notion of her plane as a phoenix; and with angry determination she stripped leather off the seats, peeled rubber from the flattened tires, and disconnected steel rods.

From twisted metal she created several essential items: cooking pots and utensils; a system of gutters, funnels, troughs, and spouts to deliver water from the running stream directly to a man-made reservoir near her dwelling. She managed to forge a combination shovel/ax from the smashed tip of a propeller blade, and she used fragments of shattered glass as magnifying elements to kindle fires by sunlight. She salvaged the rubber life raft to use as an inflatable bed; as well as a compass, a thermos, and a canteen and two cups. From the first aid kit she took scissors, tape, gauze, and a needle. Her mechanic's tools lay strewn about the wreckage of the fuselage, and she was able to locate only her hammer, a crowbar, a few wrenches, and a single screw driver. She made certain to collect all clothes carried on board.

Amie spent many weeks bringing order to this enforced habitat, each day securing some new aspect of her livelihood from nature's informal entropy; and it was only after she'd provided for her basic needs that she took some quiet time to give thanks for her subsistence and acknowledge the awesome sovereignty of her environment.

Thankfully the struggle for survival was long past. Over time her life as a solitary had become a series of peaceful devotions, routines she performed with solicitude and genuine grace. Now, along this ancient pathway she walked each day after bathing, through the palm grove above the shoreline. Near the far end of her sweet potato patch she had to ford a stream in a mist that never really made her wet. Then, passing the banana grove uphill from her tree house, vistas of the rugged coastline gave way to sauna-like alcoves, carved out by pounding waves and centuries of erosion, now protected by fern-covered canyon walls. On a hillside covered with lantana, fresh water trickled off

74

a broad-leafed spout coming out of a tree trunk, horny and spiny as the skin of a troll.

At trail's end was the beneficent cove where Amie now made her home - a place curiously familiar and comforting. Green, moss-covered stones were cast against black lava rock, like dusky segments of an abstract memory. A place of safety: this she knew - somehow.

"There's an idiot on the beach!" cried this morning's pool side interloper.

"So you've returned," acknowledged Amie, gazing into the fronds of a tall palm nearby.

"Who is the navigator?" beseeched the parrot.

"Suppose you tell me," she encouraged.

"Poor fellow," said Buenaventura.

"As far as I know," said Amie, "I'm the only person on the island."

"He talks to himself," conversed the bird.

"Does he now?"

"And he's fascinated with every word he says."

"Some of us love hearing the sound of our own voice," she allowed.

Again the remarkable parrot had managed to present a riddle that seemed impossible for her to solve.

Chapter 2.

Face down on the beach Julian found himself examining
the remains of an antediluvian eruption.  Bleached white by the
sun and salt water, granular pieces of pumice, tiny multicolored
bits of silicon, and broken fragments of shell commingled with
minuscule segments of washed-up coral.  Shaped minute after
minute by wind and water, the sand was, at the same time, light
and dark, wet and dry.  Alive with timid sand crabs and creeping
vegetation anchored in golden drift, it felt at once hot and cold.  It
was both solid and soft.  It was earth at the edge of the water.

Still soaked to the skin from the storm, Julian lay, weak
and exhausted, but glad to be alive.  Just before dawn the storm
was at its height, and the white-capped waves were cresting at ten
to fifteen feet and pounding furiously over the reef.  Had he tried
to swim to shore just a few hours earlier, he would certainly have
drowned.

"Buenaventura!  Are you here?" Julian called.

The echo of his voice returned to him from a world full of
emptiness, but Julian remained convinced that his avis friend had
flown to safety.  Upon a distant and misty cliff side he saw birds
of many species roosting in tremendous numbers.  Perhaps there
Buenaventura had found refuge.

76

Fallen tree trunks and piles of driftwood cluttered the shoreline. Roots and creepers grew gnarled and sinewy. With needle-nosed beaks, red-footed booby birds fished the shoreline for crustaceans, while egrets and albatrosses glided upon subtle air currents and hunted for tiny black lizards that camouflaged themselves in the forest brush.

It was no longer raining, yet the clouds hung low in the canyons. Fog hid the mountain peaks and crept down the slopes to cast the trees in silhouette. Julian looked past his beached boat and out to sea, trying to delineate the horizon. A moment later, (or was it an hour?), he thought he heard the sound of a familiar, though still invisible, twin engine aircraft. This time, however, the plane was not merely circling; it was in distress. Panning the breadth of the sky he saw nothing at first, though his ears told him all he needed to know. Still concealed by the remaining clouds, the plane fumbled like a blind man in a strange room, and the fine hair on the back of Julian's neck bristled from a sudden change of energy that seemed to originate somewhere beyond time. Just then *Electra* came cutting through the clouds. Rocking and wobbling as it passed perilously overhead, Julian thought, for one split second, that he could see the pilot's face through the glass of the cockpit. It was a vaguely familiar face, a face he'd once seen in a picture, or in a dream. Or perhaps in a reflection...

Running frantically up the beach to determine where the plane might touch down, he tripped over his elongated, sopping pant legs and went sprawling, face down, onto the sand. Passing his tongue over his cracked lips he tasted a drop of his blood. He spat out sand and grit and discovered he'd chipped a tooth. As he lay prone on the beach Julian heard an impact uphill, though there was no explosion nor evidence that the downed plane was on fire. Veiled not only in fog, this exotic locale seemed to manifest some impossible schizophrenia.

Up the mountainside he struggled, determined to reach the crash site before it was too late. The humid rain forest, with its tangled overgrowth, resisted intrusion. But Julian would not be denied. He knew the survival of those on board the plane might

77

depend upon his timely arrival, and possibly his rescue was contingent with theirs.

Hardly equal to such a strenuous initial test, Julian was nearly overcome with exhaustion. He knelt down in the mud and covered his face with slender, trembling hands. Appealing to some higher power, he found himself supplicating renewed strength and clarification.

"Where am I?" he muttered. "How long was I lost at sea? Is it possible I've landed in the Marianas? Or the Carolines? Have I drifted as far as the Phoenix Islands? Kiribati? Vanuatu?"

Finding strength, he moved onward. He had to try. Lives were at stake. Possibly his own... His muscles begged for rest with each step. What if they were all dead when he reached them? Who would he tell? Such morbid thoughts were not even to be considered, he told himself. The plane had not exploded upon impact. They were *not* dead! Of course they weren't...

But once he reached the perceived crash site, he found only a clearing lush with ferns and flowers. A solitary dragonfly whirled round and round his head. Where was the plane?

*Running on line. Will repeat. Will repeat...*

Julian was immediately confronted not only with the enigma of the missing plane, but with a tumultuous landslide composed of his fears and regrets from the past. Hopes, memories, fantasies, doubts, questions, faded dreams: his emotions tumbled over him unexpectedly and pressed upon him like a rock slide, as if all the loneliness he'd ever denied demanded expression at this inopportune moment. Tears dampened his sanguine cheeks and he found himself wondering whether he might have died and was encountering an afterworld of his own making.

"She's over there," directed Buenaventura at the last possible moment before Julian lost himself conclusively to a plethora of emotional confusion.

"Where are you, BV?" he called.

"Time is on our side, Captain."

"Did you see the plane?" Julian wanted to know.

"Remember Eddie Rickenbacker!"

"The plane!" Julian insisted. "Didn't you see it go down?"

"Over there," repeated Buenaventura.

"But I'm sure I saw a plane. The engines were choking for fuel. Just like the Scoundrel's engines. I know that sound all too well. And I'm sure it came down near this spot!"

On his perch in a nearby fir tree Buenaventura turned a full somersault, then spread his wings and flew directly onto Julian's shoulder.

"Maybe I only thought I saw a plane," Julian theorized. "I might have been delirious from swimming ashore. The waves were huge and the effort took nearly all my energy. There was one brief moment when I thought I had drowned. Or that I might drown... Then, suddenly, I was face down in the sand, carried in by a wave. I looked for you, BV. But I couldn't see you. Then I heard the engines. When the plane emerged from the clouds, I thought I could see the pilot's face. Or perhaps I was confused from having had too little food and not enough water while we were lost at sea. It was several weeks, you know. At least I think it was, wasn't it, BV?"

With Buenaventura riding on Julian's left shoulder, the companions started back down the trail Julian had cleared on his frantic ascent; and at times, with his wings spread out for support and balance, it appeared that the bird was steadying his partner, the man.

For here Buenaventura was at last delivered from the indignities of human domination and returned to his element. Having spent the first year of his life performing in a four-parrot sideshow in front of the Pioneer Inn in Lahaina, he was reborn the day Woody Emory rescued him from such a degrading fate. Of course BV always felt a little out of place riding over the pipeline on Woody's shoulder, but at least with Woody he was free to live in the natural world. Since his most recent adoption, however,

BV was contemplating a rather more inclusive return to the ephemeral life.

Julian returned to the beach where he'd first swum ashore. The size of the waves had diminished considerably, and with the emergence of the sunshine the sea in the cove shone a tranquil shade of blue. The wet fronds of the palm trees glistened like cellophane, and the moist earth radiated a primal, musty scent.

During his trek up the mountainside it had become apparent to Julian that even if the island were populated it was not going to be easy to locate the inhabitants. Umbrage was dense and there were no obvious paths leading from his landing point. He would have to camp out on the beach overnight - possibly longer.

"Welcome home!" said Buenaventura.

"If nobody comes for us, I don't know what we'll do," Julian lamented.

"Easy come, easy go," said the bird.

To retrieve much needed supplies from the Scoundrel, Julian stripped off his clothes to make the swim. Reaching down to untie the laces of his deck shoes he noticed that the crystal of his Rolex watch was shattered. He held the watch to his ear, but it was not ticking. The face of the watch appeared distorted through a water bubble, and Julian saw that the hands were frozen at 7:20, the precise hour that the Scoundrel had run aground on the reef. For the castaway such an irony was devoid of humor; possibly his future had ceased to exist at that moment, and perhaps he'd even begun back-tracking into some primitive, if sublime, existence. He took off the watch and placed it inside the pocket of his perspiration-soaked shirt before wading into the water.

Once on board the Scoundrel, Julian sorted through the many items he'd purchased in Hilo. Though wet from rain and ocean surf, most items were still useable. Of course his most immediate concern was food. After weeks adrift all that remained of his stock of provisions was a can of beans, some mushroom

80

soup, half a box of oyster crackers, two dozen dried apricots, a little condensed milk, and about half a pound of Kona coffee.

Yet one thing concerned him even more than his meager food supply: the need to devise some kind of anchor for his boat. Disabled as it was, the Scoundrel remained his best hope for returning to civilization.

While he had enough chain link to reach bottom, Julian was able to find nothing on board he could employ as an anchor. Abandoning a more conventional approach, he put on his snorkel and went over the railing to assess the damages and further examine his boat's position upon the reef. To his relief the hull, of the cruiser had not been breached, but the waves generated by the storm had tossed the small boat onto the coral ring in such a way that it was now leaning precariously starboard. Julian remembered seeing four heavy steel spikes in the compartment that contained the scuba gear and he determined that he might drive these into the coral with his hammer, then chain the boat right onto the reef itself. It was worth a try.

Back on deck he took off his mask and began collecting the tools necessary for the project. Before going back into the water he fastened four lengths of chain onto various parts of the boat, then tossed the ends into the water - one off the prow, one off the stern, one off the starboard side, and the other off the port side. Ready to proceed, he spit into his mask, took up his tools, and went over the side.

Though he did stir up enough sediment to cloud his vision a bit, it was relatively easy driving the spikes into the coral. Patience and persistence prevailed, however, and it was not long before Julian was back on board his boat, pleased with his own ingenuity and secure in the opinion that his craft would not break free and drift out to sea as he watched helplessly from shore. Furthermore, the boat was a beacon for anyone who might be searching for him.

Intent upon improvising a barge, Julian collected his water containers. In a calculated act of abandon he poured out all the remaining fresh water and sealed the lids tightly so that buoyancy could be achieved. He'd seen fresh water flowing in the mountain streams, but there was of course no way of knowing if the water was contaminated by bacteria or parasites. Still, if the island water was not potable, the few swallows left in his container were not going to sustain him much longer anyway.

He began lashing together the airtight containers with nylon rope. He wrapped them with the tarpaulin and secured it. Liberating the foam rubber seat cushions from their protective plastic sheaths, he zippered his meager food supplies, as well as several flares, into waterproof envelopes for a journey over the waves to shore.

He pushed the homemade barge over the side and jumped into the water. Using the inertia of the incoming waves he guided the ferry toward land. When he finally dragged the supplies on shore he was exhausted and lay down upon the sand, breathing heavily and repeating the name of the Savior.

In burnished twilight, Robinson Crusoe Crosby busied himself preparing a shelter. He wrapped the now dry tarpaulin round the extending roots of a ten-foot diameter banyan tree, creating an enclosure with immovable supports. On the beach he lit a fire. He cooked beans and brewed coffee for his supper. Buenaventura ate the last of the oyster crackers and watched as Julian sent up a distress flare, the exile never really believing there was anybody here to see it, and BV knowing well that they were not alone.

At dawn, Julian awoke to the most glorious chorus of bird song he'd ever heard. Finches, egrets, doves, honeycreepers, hornbills, plovers, mynas: thousands of birds sang in unison, as they did each morning, to herald the coming of the light.

Excited by the feral cacophony, Buenaventura paced prodigally over his keeper's chest and stomach. The parrot blinked his eyes furiously. He spread his plumage and cocked his head to listen. In time he joined the aria.

Julian held out his finger as a perch, and the bird climbed aboard without probation. Pulling back the canvas flap of the improvised shelter, Julian poked his head outside. The sea was calm and the sun was bright. Beneath a mauve sky the Trades blew through the tops of the trees. It was a rare morning in Paradise, was it not?

Yet Julian felt overwhelmed by such unlikely circumstances. Three months ago he was passively moldering in a monotonous job, practically dead, though lacking the sense to lie down. Until this moment he'd failed to realize that, for years, he'd been desperate for a miracle, all the while never really expecting any significant change in his life. "So what am I supposed to do now?" he called out. The congregation of birds abruptly stopped their singing.

Realizing his most immediate concern was finding food and water, Julian took one of his containers to a stream he'd seen yesterday on his way up the mountainside. He filled it only halfway so it would not be too heavy to carry. As for food, he knew he'd be able to fish, but he would need vegetable sustenance as well. Without straying far from the beach or the stream he made another foray into the rain forest, this time searching for edible plants rather than phantom airplanes.

His initial quest was encouraging, for he was able to locate a patch of fully ripened raspberries and a number of fallen coconuts. He also gathered seeds shed by a kukui tree. For his part, BV collected a cache of pine nuts and spread them out upon a piece of driftwood just upshore from their encampment.

With a single blow, Julian split one of the coconuts upon a rock. Immediately he drank the sweet milk inside, for he was desperately thirsty for anything other than water. He broke open several more shells and scraped the gelatinous fruit from inside the nut, savoring both taste and texture.

Later, he took his mud stained clothes back to the stream and washed them as best he could in water that tumbled over smooth, slick stones. Back on the beach he spread his laundry over a large rock to dry.

Staring at the immutable horizon, he thought: We fear what we desire most. And courage ends up being the ability to confront that which we fear. If we spend our lives living close to the flame, we burn out quickly; but if we never test our courage, the experience of living grows tedious and meaningless.

For in the process of testing courage new dimensions are revealed. Again and again we see ourselves reflected in nature - from the social structures of the smallest insects to the power of the most awesome volcano! We are as patterned as the veins of a leaf. We are thinking cells; we are waves of light. We are the memory of variations. Ultimately, we put our peculiar charge upon existence...

Julian was now forced to either look away or go under *Lono's* hypnotic spell once and for all.

Having had recent fishing practice while adrift on board the Scoundrel, albeit with limited success, casting a line was not a totally foreign pursuit for Julian. So, baiting his hook, he walked down to the waterline. There sandpipers and plovers fed upon swarms of gnats, then frantically danced away from the incoming surf. They left lines of three-toed tracks on the wet sand, which were in turn washed away by receding water. Julian took a position on a rock not normally touched by the waves and put out his line.

And having come to the conclusion that his survival might depend upon a singular effort, Buenaventura went alone into the rain forest to search for the particular elements necessary to maintain himself. With a strong beak and powerful jaws he cracked open palm nuts. He sipped nectar and pollen with his tongue and fed upon succulents growing in the salty soil of a windswept beach. There were virtually hundreds of seeds available for him to eat, but he found he also had to ingest large amounts of a particular clay to neutralize toxins contained in some local sources of food.

As evening came Julian cooked three small mullet fish over a driftwood fire. The smoke rose into the air, and the aroma of the frying fish made his mouth salivate. The sensation surprised him, for over time he'd learned to ignore feelings of emptiness and hunger. He split open several more coconuts and collected more dark, plump raspberries. Feeling a hunger for leafy vegetables, he did not refrain from experimentation, though he had no way of knowing which plants might be edible and which might be poisonous.

84

Sitting in front of the fire and eating fish right from the skillet, Julian knew that soon he would have to undertake an exploration to determine if the windward side of the island was inhabited. It would not be an easy journey though; that much was obvious by looking at the succession of promontories he would have to traverse. Now he needed rest and fortification. His ordeal at sea had not only sapped his physical strength, it had exhausted him emotionally as well. Having spent only two days as a castaway he was still growing accustomed to the idea of survival. As he finished eating, BV flew onto a perch a few feet away.

"How are you faring?" Julian wanted to know.

"For some of us the rain forest is a hard place to make a living," concluded the bird.

"Do you like raspberries?" Julian asked. He held out one of the fruits in the palm of his hand. Buenaventura took the offering in his beak. "They're good, aren't they?" said Julian.

Once the coals of his cooking fire burned low Julian watched the twilight slowly fade. Darkness grew full, and the pervasive sounds coming from deep within the forest suggested a secret and mysterious population, still unknown. Tonight sleep would not come early, so Julian lay back on the warm sand and watched the stars emerge along the curve of the encompassing dome.

Chapter 3.

Feeling the morning dew on her bare feet was Amie's favorite sensation. And as the sun climbed above the horizon and began to warm the leeward side of the island, she walked serenely along the velveteen pathway that she had worn over time. With her she carried two hand-made baskets in which to place ripened bread fruit and bananas, mangoes, papayas, and the light green, ovid fruits from a mulberry tree. She knew exactly where to find a cluster of mabolo trees, from whose limbs she collected four-inch-round butter fruits. Prolific in season and tasting similar to peaches, Amie considered them a special treat.

From time to time she gathered elements indigenous to the rain forest to make articles necessary for her solitary lifestyle: items such as paper tree bark, from which she fashioned long-burning torches; or extra thin bamboo shoots to use as sturdy needles. She collected perfect feathers, which she sharpened with shark's teeth to make writing quills; and she harvested tumeric root for dye and ink. From the poinciana, which Amie now called 'flame of the forest,' she collected the long brown seed pods filled with pea-sized nuggets. Along with colorful dried berries, she strung the seeds on braided threads to make necklaces, bracelets, and waistbands. Often she would pick the splendid white plumeria blossoms to wear in her long hair.

But Amie's survival effort surpassed her acumen as a gatherer, for not half a mile from the place where she made her home, she discovered a long-abandoned, overgrown taro field. Over time and with dedicated labor she managed to reconstitute part of the once productive field into a high yielding farm.

At yet another location she came upon a self-perpetuating sweet potato patch and she successfully transplanted some of the tubers adjacent to the taro field. Year round she grew more than enough of the two distinct roots for her needs.

In mid-afternoon Amie took her nets to the enclosed, pearly green fish breeding pond that she'd reconstructed during her second year as a foundling. Bordered by lava rock, succulents, and a few patches of reeds, fresh water flowed from underground and mixed with ocean tides, allowing a unique system of aqua culture to develop and thrive.

Amie spent long hours diligently studying the food chain in order to maximize a marine harvest. She deduced that bacteria and other micro-organisms broke down organic matter into nutrients that were recycled back into the pond. Photosynthesis enabled the phytoplankton and seaweed to use the nutrients for growth. The zooplankton ate these plants, as well as larger fishes. Young, small fish entered the lagoon from the sea through a grate of poles set in the channel that connected the smaller pond to the sea. Grazing on algae, plankton, and small shrimp, the small fishes would grow too large to escape back through the grate into the sea. Amie was able to take many varieties from the pond, including mullet, surgeon fish, goby, scad, and eels. Carnivores such as barracudas and jacks were at the top of the food chain.

Amie lowered her hand-tied net as she surveyed the familiar surroundings. Tall coconut palms, iridescent when cast against the backdrop of gathering clouds, nearly obscured the volcanic mountain in the distance. The tops of the palm trees flapped like banners in the breeze and glistened like diamond-studded tiaras. Their long, ringed trunks, bulbous at their base in the sand, or shackled by the debris of peeled bark - some charcoal gray, some bleached white - supported splendid botanical corollas. Seed pods looked like swarms of bees.

Behind the palms grew the twisted trunks of a colony of deciduous trees, the entire population shaped by prevailing patterns of wind and light. Here they remained unchallenged by malevolent forces, for no man-made order presumed to impose. Conventional time was easily dismissed.

Billowy clouds promoted expanded self-image and provided a backdrop so one did not forever discount the world of forms. Indeed, such a thing might happen if Amie were to define herself solely within temporal rhythms. South Seas surrealism enclosed this beach, this forest, and this lagoon inside a protective bubble where deep relaxation was not only possible, but wholly unavoidable. Amie no longer felt any panic at venturing out-of-body, beyond clouds and mountains, over waves to meet a timeless horizon; overcoming gravity, too, until time itself ceased to have meaning - or perhaps until it began to flow backwards - or until she glimpsed the future - or eternity itself! This environment was pure sweetness. It was a velvet touch upon the skin. With such ease she became lost in the ecstasy.

"The Scoundrel's on the reef!"

Startled by the voice of a recent acquaintance, Amie's attention returned to the present as BV swooped down and landed on a nearby rock.

"You keep showing up at the most unexpected moments," Amie observed through a smile.

"The captain's out of sorts!"

"How so?" she asked.

"Dysentery," said the bird woefully.

As Amie cast her net into the pond, BV darted from tree to tree. Attempting to command her undivided attention, he spoke to her in compelling riddles.

Amie listened as he chattered on endlessly about the invalid captain and the Scoundrel. Having taken not a single fish from the pond, she decided she must pull her net from the water at once.

88

Away from the shore and up a pathway that led over the north-facing promontory, Amie followed Buenaventura's course. Through the steamy forest she hiked, knee-deep in soft ferns, a canopy of dracaenas overhead. Delicate orchids grew upon fallen, water-soaked limbs. Red and yellow-leafed crotons, along with prolific stands of torch ginger, marked her line of ascent up the cliff side. And waiting restlessly for her at each turn was the intensely provocative budgie.

Reaching the top of the incline, where the vista spread over inlet and seashore, Amie first noticed the wrecked ship upon the coral reef. Her reaction was not one of joy - or fear. Rather it was one of confusion.

Crouching behind a large rock and surveying the shoreline, she noticed the tarpaulin wrapped round the extending roots of the banyan tree. Upon the yellow sand she observed the charred remains of a fire. Strewn near the shelter were a number of articles: the water tanks; tools; a few pieces of clothing. Amie could barely distinguish two bare feet sticking out of the tent.

After so many years alone, how could she consider *not* risking contact? Early on, (before she'd grown decidedly accustomed to solitude), she would have been glad to come across anybody, for there were times she thought she might literally die of loneliness. Her legacy was one sadly destitute of expression.

Buenaventura perched upon an extending branch very close to Amie's ear. "There's an idiot on the beach," he croaked again.

"Is it a man or a woman?" Amie asked.

"The only man in a forgotten world," lamented the bird.

"What about the boat?" Amie wanted to know.

"Hopeless," said BV.

"What's wrong with it?"

"Bogus carburetors..."

"Can't they be fixed?" she wanted to know.

"Only Kamehaloha," said Buenaventura.

"Is that the man's name?" Amie asked.

"Give me a pine nut!" said the parrot.

Amie continued to watch the castaway from her coverture on top of the promontory, all the while hoping he would come out of his tent and show his face. Growing increasingly excited by the prospect of contact with another human, she also cultivated reticence. What if he was deranged or violent? What if he was the carrier of some appalling, communicable disease?

"Did you also arrive on the boat?" she asked BV.

"Alas, set adrift over uncertain seas!"

"From where did you sail?"

"Captain Cook - what a crook!"

"You mean you came all the way from Hawaii?"

"*Aloha*... Surf's up... Through the pipeline..."

"If we're near the Hawaiian chain..." Amie speculated. "No, that's impossible! *Electra* never had enough fuel to stay airborne all the way to Hawaii!"

"This is *Electra* calling *Itasca*. We are running on line. Will repeat. Will repeat..."

"Where did you learn that?"

"*Merciless life laughs in the burning sun...*"

"That's my poem!" she protested.

Repeating a previous inquiry, BV challenged, "What are *you* doing here?" Ruffling his feathers and cocking his head, he waited to hear Amie's reply.

"I told you, I was marooned here a long time ago."

"He heard the crash, you know," Buenaventura volunteered.

"Impossible," said Amie. "That was long, long ago."

"The Scoundrel's on the reef!" BV blasted.

"And I arrived here on the wings of a dragonfly," she said with a playful glint in her eye.

"Impossible!" shrieked the bird.

"No more impossible than you drifting here all the way from Hawaii..."

"Anchor's gone. Too bad!" BV shook his head and clicked his tongue inside his beak.

"You must understand," she told the bird, "I've been on my own for years and years. I need time!"

90

"We're all out of time," reminded BV.

"Don't worry," said Amie, "I *will* help him. You'll see my torch in the forest after dark. Then you'll know I'm on my way..."

Buenaventura flew down to the beach to keep a vigil over Julian, while Amie hiked over the palisade to her home near the great banana grove. BV was not inclined to detail his meeting with Amie to Julian, and even had he been disposed to do so, his companion was in no condition to converse.

Throughout the afternoon Amie felt the lively fluttering of a thousand butterflies in her stomach. Nervous as a schoolgirl, she assessed her bright and youthful face in the mirror above her outdoor, tortoise-shell basin.

As twilight cast mountain, grove, and coastline in honeyed hyalescence, she assembled the items she wished to bring for the castaway. Besides a basketful of fruit and flowers, she packed a blanket made of tapa cloth and decorated with her own drawings of tropical images, as well as one of her own frond-woven sun hats. Amie also gathered together the peculiar components for the administering of *awa*.

She waited for darkness before setting off on her journey. Through the pulsating forest she moved, climbing with little effort to the top of the protected ridge. A glowing torch lighted the way she knew from memory. Her handmade, wood frame backpack rested squarely upon her shoulders, and it was only half an hour before she approached the desolate beach where Julian had landed just three days before.

Buenaventura saw the light from Amie's torch as she drew near and flew to meet her where the sylvan slopes of the promontory descended toward the shore. Landing on top of her carrier, he admonished her for taking so long. "The captain's out of sorts," registered the caretaker.

"I know, dysentery... Don't worry, I have everything necessary to put him right."

"He doesn't look well," said BV doubtfully.

91

"You must understand," she told the parrot, "such a purge is to be expected for one coming out of civilization into a world so undefiled."

"*Kahuna* knows best," BV allowed.

Amie crossed the sand expecting a welcome from the island's newest tenant. He did not present himself. Stopping near the improvised shelter, and not knowing whether there was really someone inside the tent, she called out hesitantly, "Hello... Is anybody there?"

No response. She again made overture. "I'm here to help," she said. "No need to remain hidden."

Still, no reply... What was she to do?

BV perched nearby, and Amie looked to him for advice. "You should go inside,"he declared. "I'm afraid he's fallen unconscious."

Amie planted her torch in the sand and approached the sanctuary. It was not her wish to violate anyone's privacy, but now she feared something was terribly wrong. Just for a moment she was overcome with a sense of panic... What if she had not come in time? What if he was beyond help? Or what if he was already dead? No! Such irony would be too cruel.

Cautiously she drew back the flap and peered inside the tent. By the light of the flickering cresset she observed a middle-aged Caucasian man, prone and looking pallid and quite emaciated. Perspiration covered his forehead, and his purple lips were swollen and cracked. He was shivering. With eyes rolled back, he coughed weakly then muttered something unintelligible. Judging the situation critical, Amie went immediately to his side.

*Awa* was good when one was exhausted. After laboring day and night - diving, paddling, stooping, pulling - she had taken this cure herself! The *awa* had to be chewed, and to that end she was obliged to help the invalid. Then the heads of fishes were unwrapped from ti leaf sheaths. A bunch of dead-ripe bananas, some sour cane, and sweet potatoes - ringed in shape and deep red in color - was each presented and blessed. More *awa* was strained through fibers. Water was added and the dregs were squeezed until there was no fluid left. She poured the vile potion down his throat, and the patient gagged.

"Sorry for the nausea," she said. "It's necessary."

"My ears are ringing," he swooned.

"The whistling in your ears is the sound of land shells. It is the roaring resonance of your exile. Now, slip into peace and contentment. Feel the lightness of your being. Roll with the waves of your destiny."

*At the Sunrise on Maui, Julian was on familiar ground again. He stared inquisitively at Song Cajudoy as she poured him guava juice. "This one's on the house," she said.*

*"Thanks." said Julian. He drank down half a glassful immediately. "The taste is luxurious," he sighed.*

*"Don't mention it."*

*"I think it's the sweetness I miss most," he confided.*

*The Filipina smiled paradoxically. "Everybody wants to taste sweetness," she said.*

*Kamehaloha was lounging at his usual table. Sleepy-eyed, he stared across the water at Lanai Island. Tamara Sly was with him, looking lovely as always.*

*"Aloha, brother!"*

*"Hello, Kamehaloha. Hello, Tamara."*

*"Are you taking good care of the Scoundrel?" asked the Hawaiian.*

*"I'm having a little trouble with the carburetors," Julian related. "Perhaps you can give me some advice."*

*Kamehaloha shook his head. "It's all a matter of balance and flow, Julian. Keep working with them. You'll master it. I have confidence in you..."*

*"Thanks, Kamehaloha."*

*Tamara crossed her bare legs and her sarong fell away from her knee and thigh. Julian held his breath as she looked at him with limpid eyes and said, "Why didn't you wait for me in Hilo, Julian?"*

*"I did wait," he told her. "I thought you went with Woody."*

*"I was coming," she laughed. "You didn't give me time!"*

*"I guess we're all out of time. Sorry," he said. And he really was...*

*Suddenly everything changed. Along with the familiar and comfortable surroundings at the Sunrise, the images of friends faded like shadows in twilight, and Julian found himself exiting his body through a tear duct in the corner of his right eye.*

*And carrying the weight of long-felt resentment upon scrawny shoulders, he marched to a place near the volcano's cinder cone, where Polynesians had once performed sacrifices. He knew he must throw off all feelings of bitterness and regret. Kamehaloha called him* haole. *Perhaps that was appropriate after all.*

*Deep inside a cave his spirit lover presented him with a wood-carved talisman to wear around his neck; and by the light of a blazing fire she told him they would have great adventures together, hereafter only under the cover of darkness. They did* not *become intimate in their dreams, but rather their dreams became intimate.*

Next morning Julian awoke long after daybreak. Inside his tent he felt disoriented, as if he'd had too much to drink the night before. Of course that was impossible. There was no alcohol here. He remembered the initial stages of his illness - the waves of nausea, the desperation, fever, and weakness. Apparently the dysentery was over now. Though his stomach still hurt and his muscles ached. Carefully he sat upright. Looking for his shirt, he became aware of a small, carved figure hanging by a braided string round his neck. Of course he had no idea from where it had come. Yet he felt a certain degree of familiarity with the amulet. Then he noticed a basketful of fruit and flowers near the doorway. What was this?

Along with the gift was a short note written on paper thin bark in red ink:

94

"Dear Unfortunate Companion,

Apparently your poor sense of direction rivals my own. Nevertheless, I bid you welcome. When you wake, meet me where the mountain stream flows into the Seven Sisters. The parrot will escort you there.

Amie"

Excited, Julian scrambled out of his tent. During the night some Good Samaritan had found him in distress and left an offering of friendship, as well as an invitation. Perhaps his exile would soon end.

He took a mango from the basket, peeled it, and began eating. The succulent flesh of the fruit and the sweet juice tantalized his taste buds like no food he'd eaten before. Though he'd not been habituated to sugar in the past, Julian found himself craving sweetness, as a bee deprived of pollen. What might once have seemed insipid now provided the ultimate nourishment. Finishing the mango, he immediately began on passion fruit. After that, star fruit and papayas.

He danced a happy little dance on the warm sand, but quickly realized he was not yet fully recovered from illness. Feeling dizzy, he sat down to reconstruct as best he could the chain of events leading up to this glorious moment. There was the landing. And the dubious plane crash... Evidently BV was fending for himself without difficulty. And what had he eaten that made him so sick? Was it the mullet fish? The berries? Or was it the combination of bitter greens he'd made into a salad?

"Buenaventura! Buenaventura! Where are you?" he called. "Come out of the trees, my friend. Good news! Good news! We're not alone after all!"

Chapter 4.

Having spent her entire life with her keeper in Manhattan, the captive one day discovered her wings were never clipped. Taking to delirious flight within the confines of the apartment, she came upon an unexpected reflection. Totally absorbed by the ecstasy of meeting one of her kind, she flew headlong into the harsh reality of the bathroom mirror. Stunned, she collapsed into the basin, a pathetic heap of bones and ruffled feathers. A powerful stream of water from the spigot pummeled her as she fluttered helplessly upon slippery porcelain. Nearly submerged and starting to lose consciousness, she slipped into a long, black tunnel, only to awaken some time later in a splendid place, previously unknown to her. Instinctively she knew she was finally home, but home alone.

Now concealed amidst a crop of cool green ferns she waited impatiently near the massive down-sloping clay field. There she'd observed the blue and yellow macaw twice before, and she knew he must come again to ingest the particular red clay necessary to neutralize food toxins.

True to her prediction he came at last to the mud field. The female watched as he clawed at the ground and dipped his beak into the grit. His head bobbed as he swallowed the clay. He clawed again, ruffled his wings, spread out his tail feathers. When he'd ingested enough of the clay he flew away. Never out of her sight, he landed in an acacia tree. There he began sipping nectar with his tongue from the tree's yellow flowers. From her perch she flew to meet him.

"*It's about time...*" she addressed him.

Surprised to come across another of his kind, he acknowledged, "It's the nature of this place."

"Have you always been here? " she wanted to know.

"Shipwrecked," he said. "How about you?"

"I once lived in New York City," she told him.

"What happened?"

"That life went down the drain," she said.

Buenaventura knew something about abrupt changes and found no need to inquire further as to the means of her arrival. For he felt as if he'd come upon some part of himself that he'd not previously recognized as missing. Mutual destiny became their rite and purpose. "What are you called?" he wanted to know.

"I am Jewel," she said simply.

"And I am Buenaventura!"

Two spirits had been released from the confinement of a linear world and delivered into one of beauty and bliss - a world made on the first day of Creation for their specific rendezvous. At once theirs was a magisterial relationship, aphoristic since the beginning of time.

Compelled to practice the manifold rituals of courtship, yet understanding all along that ritual must ultimately give way to preordination, they soared above canyons and waterfalls and took harborage from inclement weather inside tree hollows and cliff side rock notches. They explored every demarcation of their new home: its sounds; its smells; its topography. They played the game of flight and pursuit. They cooed and preened, and she slept beneath the warm and protective cover of his wing.

"We don't need the humans anymore, Buenaventura," Jewel observed.

"But without us they are probably helpless," he said.

"What is it about them?"

"They won't give themselves away. They remain hidden behind artifice."

"Why?" Jewel wished to know.

"Because they're frightened of currents and draughts and storms. Over and over again they make themselves empty amidst a world of plenty."

"But they act so superior," said Jewel.

"It's true," BV conceded. "That's because they don't realize that every other species sees through their duplicity."

Chapter 5.

Cut off by the impenetrable forest and steep mountains, Julian paced up and down the shoreline bitterly muttering to himself about the Scoundrel's infernal carburetors, about his ineptitude as a sailor, and about the obvious limits of his beach front encampment. Knowing another was somewhere present on the island, yet having made no contact with his benefactor, only reinforced his sense of isolation to the point of despair. He ate the fruit left for him by Amie, and he fished.

"Buenaventura!"

His outcry tumbled back at him from the wall of the escarpment at the end of the beach. The note left by Amie promised that the parrot would help him locate her, but Julian had not seen the bird for days. Where was he?

In frustration Julian sat on the sand with his back against a rock and looked out to sea. How vast the ocean was! Cast adrift for two weeks without bearing he'd not fully comprehended its enormity. Suddenly he was aware of his diminutive position.

"Water, water, every where,
And all the boards did shrink;
Water, water, every where,
Nor any drop to drink."

99

Like the Mariner, he'd killed the Albatross, his arrow being default.

No effort at reconciliation was made as Kelly slammed the door on their marriage; no protest lodged as Kirsten ran like a refugee for Seattle; and no rally mounted on his behalf by co-workers in an attempt to save his job. Nor had he the courage to entice Tamara Sly with all her ambidextrous possibilities... Truly a castaway before the fact, Julian had been seduced by a Siren of the Sea then set adrift to pitch and roll with the current. Sucked into the vortex of enigma he was now the prisoner of his own feckless initiative.

Amie appointed her particular charge to everything within this tropical capsule. Here she was supreme goddess. Yet with the arrival of the man, she realized, a critical plurality had been reached. In time he would compromise her influence, abridge her power. The balance would shift.

It had been three days and still he had not come to her. Perhaps she should not have entrusted the fickle parrot to guide him to her encampment, but from the start Amie knew she could not be the one to approach. She climbed to the top of the promontory and hid herself amidst the rocks and foliage. From her belvedere she watched as he sat, motionless, on the beach, looking out to sea. Perhaps she understood how he was feeling. In time he would come to terms with the fact that there was no escape. The island's mutable validity would ultimately impose itself upon his attitude. One grew accustomed to abstractions.

I have learned to be my own best friend, thought Amie to herself. Until now I have been all things human to this domain and I have come to cherish the harmony I impart. Would it be selfish to wish for peaceful continuity?

She left her reconnaissance post and walked through the banana grove to the place where the pure waters of the Seven Sisters consoled her uncertainties and replenished her inner beauty. Today she bathed in the last of the descending pools, for the water in this pondlet was the warmest of the cascade.

On this Pacific atoll loneliness synthesized its own peculiar sound - one that emanated from deep within Julian's temperament.    First  perceived  as  distant  thunder,  these reverberations flowed up from his solar plexus and into his chest. They rattled his rib cage and surrounded his heart.  Not a single drop of replenishing rain moistened his sunburned, parched lips.

And had Amie not come to him in his time of desolation and illness, suicide might now be a serious consideration.  Indeed, what a pathetic legacy his human bones would make!  Julian took up a handful of sand and sifted the white granules through his open fingers, and it occurred to him that each falling grain defined the retreat of sovereign possibilities.  If only this friend called Amie would reveal herself...

The full moon rose behind him and cast its glow upon the crests of the incoming waves.  Stars swirled overhead, while the tide ebbed and flowed to incomprehensible rhythms.  In a single breath Julian exhaled everything he'd once assumed true.

Amie lay on her inflatable life raft bed, the same rubber raft she'd salvaged long ago from the wreckage of the *Electra*. Now she seldom thought about the crash, nor about her airplane. Not inclined to retrace her steps, Amie focused intently upon the present.  She contemplated the yellow moon in the indigo sky; she bathed herself in the sentient breeze; she watched geckoes climb bamboo  curtains  half-lowered  on  the  windward  side  of  her structure.

Yes, it was a beautiful tropical night, but Amie was restless.  Naked, she tossed and wrangled beneath her woven mat. It was a night filled with fantasies; torpid dreams; forgotten lust; fires cooled by loss of polarity, then suddenly, surprisingly rekindled; pleasures abandoned for the sake of emotional survival, now precipitously recalled.

Tonight Amie was aware of her body.  Try as she might she could not relax.  She ran her hands over her warm stomach, felt the fullness of her breasts, followed the lines of her waist and hips.  Her inhalations grew deeper and deeper.  In the darkness

Amie self-consciously touched her femininity and felt the humid warmth of her first menstruation since coming to Paradise.

Chapter 6.

"Muster up!  You're looking rather pathetic, Captain!"
said a voice from over Julian's shoulder.

He turned to find the bird perched on a nearby limb.
"Where have you been?" he wanted to know.  "I haven't seen you
for days!"

"Whirlwind romance," answered the familiar.

"You?" inquired Julian.

"Imagine the ego," said BV.  "Do you think humans are
the only creatures on earth who appreciate a pretty face?"

"Of course not, but..."

"Tamara Sly was half your age, Captain, but I
volunteered not one word of criticism."

"What makes you think I had it for Tamara Sly?" Julian
kidded.

"Most humans don't realize it," BV needled, "but when
they're sexually aroused they give off an unmistakable mating
scent.  Not to mention the fact that they get a shamefully guilty
look in their eyes.  As a species it's impossible for you to watch
yourselves: you're far too egocentric.  But if you *could* see
yourselves I think you'd be terribly embarrassed."

"You don't say," said Julian cynically.

Just then Jewel flew up to join her mate.

"Julian," said Buenaventura, "this is Jewel."

Quite surprised, Julian came face-to-face with BV's vibrant mate for the first time. "The pleasure is all mine, I'm sure."

"Sometimes his attitude seems rather condescending," BV told Jewel, "but he means no harm."

She seemed prepared to accept BV's human comrade without proviso. "Perhaps it's time we lead him to Amie..." Her suggestion could not have been more welcome.

Guided by the two macaws, Julian climbed the south-facing promontory, up a path he'd not previously noticed. The morning was gray and steamy as he moved to initiate his redemption. Sweat poured off his brow. His heartbeat was wild, though his breath was strong.

Hopefully the apex of this five-hundred-foot hill would become the apogee between maddening isolation and fellowship; for apparently a covenant had been conceived, with or without his conscious consent, between the remote, esoteric woman, Amie, and himself. Of course Julian was grateful for her kind and able ministrations during his illness, still he could not imagine who or what he might find at the end of this trail.

Descending the promontory through sauna-like alcoves, he emerged around a final outcropping of large, moss-covered boulders. Crossing over a stream he entered the perimeter of Amie's enclave. The rough-hewn home site certainly fascinated Julian, yet he was disgruntled as well. For he'd fervently hoped to come across some sort of community, not another castaway like himself!

Respectfully he approached the house. He called out a greeting but nobody answered. He walked round and round Amie's tree house, noting various improvised conveniences: the rope ladders made from banyan vines; the bamboo shades and palm-thatched roof with leafy shingles; the intricate system of gutters fashioned to deliver water from the stream. Judging from the relative sophistication of her house, she'd lived here for some time. Apparently there was much she could teach him about survival on the island, but generally Julian found the evidence of her longtime residency disheartening. He certainly did not plan to spend the rest of his life here!

With cupped hands he drank from Amie's reservoir. Having quenched his thirst he ventured uphill from the house. He discovered the banana grove and picked one of the fruits to eat. She was living a life of comparative abundance while he waited on the beach for rescue, famished and expiring. He wondered why she'd not approached him sooner. Why such reticence? Why such mystery?

Amidst his parade of speculations he almost failed to distinguish her as she came walking up the Seven Sisters path. As shafts of sunlight filtered through the tops of the trees, highlighting her long, curly hair, Julian beheld Amie for the first time. Slim and lithe, she was radiant as an emerald, and he blinked his eyes thinking he might be inventing such a creature. But Amie was no mirage. The perfect manifestation of her environment, her smooth face was without tension. Graceful arms descended to pliant hands and elegant, slender fingers. Her hips were girlish and her legs were long and muscular. She appeared strong and agile, decidedly feminine.

Through gray-green eyes she seemed to be shamelessly apprising some aspect of his bearing beyond contemporary understanding. Julian, in turn, thought he recognized her from some other place. But where? Then he remembered: The girl whose reflection he'd seen in the tide pool on Maui had implored him to subscribe to a timeless, recurrent reverie.

"Welcome," she said. Her voice was deeper than he might have expected.

"You must be Amie..." Julian stood up and began to move toward her. The suddenness of his advance startled her, and she recoiled. He stopped. "My name is Julian Crosby," he offered.

"Are you well now?" she wanted to know.

"Completely recovered, thanks to you."

"When I found you, you were dangerously dehydrated," she told him.

"How did you know I was there?" he asked.

"The blue macaw led me to you."

Julian craved contact from the deepest part of his entity, yet he was receiving signals imposing restraint. Each watched, waited, speculated in silence. On a nearby limb BV and Jewel sat side by side.

"This might sound like a stupid question," Julian said, "but what is this place?"

"I don't honestly know," said Amie.

"Are there any other people here?" Julian wanted to know.

"No one else," she said.

"Are you certain?"

"Yes..." She was hoping he would soon give up the inquisition so she might simply be his friend.

"Have you explored the entire island?"

She nodded. "There's nobody else here. We're all alone."

"How did you get here?"

"Same as you," she said.

"Shipwreck?"

"She nodded almost imperceptibly.

"How long have you been here?"

Amie shrugged her shoulders. "I'm not sure," she said.

"What about your boat?" he asked.

"Gone," was all she offered.

The expression on Julian's face was dubious. He motioned to the clearing where Amie's home stood. "You've made quite a comfortable life for yourself," he observed.

"In the beginning I was like you. I slept on the beach. I weathered storms. I waited to be rescued."

"But nobody came," he finished in a low voice.

"I cried and cried. I lit a fire on the beach. For weeks I never let it go out. I watched and watched until the horizon disappeared. Not a single ship. During the time I've been here, I've never seen a plane fly overhead."

106

"Right after I swam ashore I thought I saw a plane crash on the mountainside," Julian related. "I ran through the forest to the place where I saw it disappear. But when I arrived, there was nothing but a lone dragonfly circling and circling."

"A Calico Pennant," she determined.

"A what?"

"They're the best flyers in the world."

"Then I only thought I saw a plane..."

A protracted silence intruded on the conversation. Finally she said, "If you are hungry, I will make you some food."

It was a good suggestion. And they walked, not side by side, the short distance to Amie's house.

Again Julian examined the castaway as she scrubbed tubers and peeled wild onions to bake with lemon grass inside her stone oven. Her lips were full and her cheekbones high. Her deep tan hid what would otherwise have been a field of freckles. Sandy eyebrows framed emotive eyes. She moved with the grace and agility of one well adapted to such circumstances.

"Where did your journey originate?" Julian asked.

"New Guinea," she said.

Showing astonishment Julian conjectured, "We must be quite far south..."

"The island is situated very near the equator," Amie informed him.

"I have nautical maps," Julian offered.

Amie only shrugged. "I don't suppose they'll do us much good without a serviceable craft," she observed dispassionately.

His enthusiasm fell slightly. "I presume you have observed the full range of seasons," he said.

"Many times," she indulged him.

Having flavored the sweet potatoes with herbs and extracts, Amie moved to her oven and prepared to make a fire using a piece of convex glass and a bit of reflective material salvaged long ago. Observing the process, Julian offered her a match. She smiled tolerantly. "I don't need those," she said. Once the fire was kindled and the crock of vegetables was cooking, Amie prepared a luxurious fruit salad. As she washed, peeled, and sliced the fruit she could see that her guest was quite hungry. When the mixture was ready she offered the repast. Julian accepted the compote and immediately began to savor the sweetness.

"I have a number of useful items," he told her. Of course he was referring to materials he had taken off the Scoundrel.

Again Amie looked at him curiously. Obviously, she was in need of very little. "I saw the debris from your boat strewn over the beach where you landed," she said.

"I still have to get things organized," he explained.

Amie found his feigned confidence rather ingratiating. "Survival does not come easily at first," she told him. "Only when you finally give up resistance will you begin to live in harmony with your fate. It's not so bad if you can stand the solitude," she said.

"Have you stopped hoping for rescue?" he asked.

"I seldom think about it anymore."

"I think of nothing else," he related.

"Of course that will pass..."

"But I don't want it to pass. I never want to lose hope!"

"Hope infers a future," Amie said. "Time is different here, Julian. You'll see."

After their meal Amie gave him two torches for light, a woven basket in which to collect fruit, and a bamboo mat for sleeping. She also offered him a feather quill, ink, and paper tree bark for writing. She showed him where he could find butter fruit and ginger. She took him to see her taro field and her sweet potato patch.

"Where did you get the metal to construct your water system?" he wanted to know.

"Washed ashore," she said vaguely.

Amie was intensely proud of her fish pond and she tried to educate Julian about the principles that sustained it. Together they walked out upon the rocks that formed the pond's perimeter. Amie's ingenuity and adaptability impressed Julian. "You are welcome to take fish from my pond," she told him. "And if you would like, I will help you construct one of your own."

At that moment Julian realized he would soon be going back over the hill to his own wretched encampment and a pervasive feeling of separation began to move over him like an accustomed memory. Apparently exclusivity was not reason enough for immediate affinity.

Julian began fingering the talisman which Amie had placed around his neck. The amulet depicted a single point amidst a vast field. "What is the meaning of this?" Julian asked.

"A symbol to represent the truth of our predicament."

"And what truth is that?"

Placing her hand upon his shoulder, Amie made physical contact for the first time. Her touch was reassuring in the most profound way imagineable. "We are alone in Paradise," she whispered.

Chapter 7.

Having learned from the female solitary that they were alone on this tropical atoll and that the chance for rescue was remote, Julian might well have felt depressed and hopeless. He did not. He penetrated his fear for the time being and focused upon personal qualities often relegated to a background position in his personality - resolve and tenacity. For after seeing Amie's marvelous domicile he awoke next morning determined to make the best of his exile.

Dismantling his first island home, he began constructing a permanent shelter made of bamboo poles and palm fronds. Such a house would allow the northeast breeze to blow freely through the porous hut, cooling torpid skin and calming nighttime anxieties.

From fallen wood found in the forest he constructed a small table and two chairs. Using the nails and screws he'd bought in Hilo, he built shelves on which to store salvaged supplies. Upon one particular shelf Julian placed a line of hollowed-out coconut shells. Inside the shells he collected the pieces of an obscure puzzle - unlikely items somehow deemed vital to his survival: nuts and berries; colorful stones; dragonfly wings for Amie; fish scales; colored sand; beetles; lures; feathers; patches of shirt material; his broken Rolex watch; rain water.

"Captain's gone *tropo!*" crowed BV.

Julian was weaving a hammock from fronds.

"Jewel's with Amie," BV related.

"That's nice," said Julian.

"You know you want to see her again."

"Of course I do..."

"No time like the present, Captain."

"I'm busy now, Buenaventura. This is important work." Julian tied one final knot securing the hammock to koa wood supports, then proclaimed, "Now it's time for fishing. How about keeping me company, Buenaventura?"

The parrot flew away reciting pre-Colombian poetry:

"We only come here to sleep,
We only come here to dream.
It is not true, it is not true,
That we come to Earth to live."

With her heaviest fishing net slung across her shoulders, Amie hiked three miles over hill and through dense forest until she descended to a beach front that she'd named Turtle Cove. Each evening a hundred sea turtles came here to bob and swim in the undulating surf. Normally Amie came only to observe and commune with these animals, but tonight her purpose was more diabolical. She slipped off her sandals and placed them on dry sand before walking cautiously over slippery black stones to a point where she could watch the creatures as they surfaced for air. Not often did she come to diminish their number, but this evening she meant to cast her net in hopes of capturing one of the sea turtles.

In truth, the cumbersome creatures were an easy catch, and on her fourth casting Amie netted a small tortoise. A tear of affection formed in her eye. Clutching her net tightly with work-strengthened hands, she begged forgiveness as she dragged the heavy sea turtle ashore. Once off the slippery rocks and on the sandy beach, she turned the unfortunate animal on its back. There it lay, helpless, as Amie disentangled her net.

111

Unfortunately the animal would not die immediately, but Amie knew of no humane way to effect a kill. When the sun came out tomorrow morning the turtle would retreat inside its shell and, unable to right itself, eventually expire. Then Amie would return to harvest her catch.

She returned home in waning light reflected off billowy, ocean-borne clouds and bathed underneath a dome of stars. By torch light Amie stood before her mirror, visually sculpting her figure - practically willing vision into flesh, fantasy into form. Her youthful face grew more lovely, her hair more shiny. Her lips seemed fuller, her eyes clearer. Her lucid expression suggested innocence peppered with a bit of longing. Her skin was luxuriant. Not since she was a newborn, cradled in her mother's arms, had Amie known the security of such perfect physical harmony.

With Buenaventura riding upon his right shoulder, Julian started over the promontory bearing a small gift of several fishing lures. He realized this bantam offering was hardly recompense for the help and encouragement Amie had already provided him, but, in truth, he had little she might need. He found the trail difficult as the stitching on his deck shoes was beginning to unravel and fray. Also, one of the soles had become dislodged and was flapping with each step he took. His gate looked silly and uneven as he crossed the meridian and began the descent toward Amie's compound.

Who is this woman, he wondered, stranded like myself in a forgotten place? During their first and only meeting he had asked question after question, but come away with little information.

She possessed the candid face of a muse. He'd noticed at once that her hands were loveliest at task. And while he hungered for contact, he was not certain on which dynamic to begin. When Julian entered her encampment he found that she was not there.

"She's probably with the Seven Sisters," suggested BV. "She goes there each morning to commune."

"Can you guide me there?" asked Julian.

"Follow the yellow brick road," instructed the parrot.

Julian wandered through the banana grove to the place where he had first met Amie. There he located the path on which she'd entered the stand. He continued up the gentle incline, tracing the conformation of the path side stream. Coming to a clearing, he saw the first of the seven descending pools. Immersed in clear, sparkling water, and quite unaware of his presence, Amie swam, naked.

At first he said nothing, for he did not want to startle her. Taken with her rare beauty, he watched as her head and sun-dappled shoulders emerged above the waterline. Droplets shone like tiny gems as they fell from her face back into the pool. Her fingertips moved a few stray hairs away from closed eyelids. Lifting her arms and opening her palms toward the sun, Amie invoked the spirits to preserve her in a place she had come to cherish.

Opening her eyes, Amie saw him watching her. She smiled shyly and slipped beneath the water, up to her chin. Julian surveyed the seven pools that descended from the ninety-foot waterfall. "So this is the place you call the Seven Sisters?"

"It's appropriate, don't you think so?"

"It's very beautiful here," said Julian reverently.

"I would have brought you here eventually," she said.

"I don't mean to intrude," he said, certainly not wanting to withdraw.

"The water's fine," said Amie. " Would you like to swim?"

"If you wouldn't mind," said Julian.

Perched upon a palm branch, Buenaventura regarded the scene from a higher perspective. "Situation's critical," he cautioned.

Of course Julian was inclined to discount BV's warning.

"He's an absolute delight!" said Amie.

"Sometimes he's a real killjoy!"

Amie instructed Julian to find a large, round stone, wrap a broad ti leaf around it, and place it with the other stones upon the pool side altar she'd created long ago as an offering to the serpent god, Mo'o. Julian felt somewhat foolish, and asked, "Is that necessary?"

"It is unless you want to be pulled down to the bottom to spend eternity..."

Julian smiled. Carrying out the prescribed ritual was a small price to pay for a skinny-dip in this idyllic pool with the siren of any man's fancy.

"Take off all your clothes," Amie instructed.

Julian wasted little time doing as he was told. Off came his tattered shoes, his rumpled shirt, his torn, sagging pants. Amie drew him into the water with her rapt expression.

Immersing himself in the pool, Julian felt an unaccustomed intensity, and he shuddered.

"Are you cold?" Amie asked.

"No, it's something else," he said. "Something quite different."

Amazed by a sudden and totally unexpected surge of effervescence, Julian was at a loss to explain such a feeling. Perhaps he was stronger, more virile. But how could such a thing be true? It seemed to him as if years had been instantly washed away. His thoughts and visions became increasingly volatile, his spirit more resilient. Bewildered by such feelings of conjunction with the physical circumstances around him, Julian looked to Amie for an explanation.

"Quite extraordinary, isn't it?" she said.

"Yes, but *what* is it? What are these feelings?"

"How can I explain?" she said gently.

"Please try!" Julian searched the periphery of the environment like a man whose mind and body were suddenly capable of anything.

"I'm not sure I understand completely," said Amie.

"But after all this time you must!"

"What if all we have to do is offer stones and innocence, and this pool renders visions of immortality?"

"How can it be?" asked Julian incredulously.

"Perhaps we who live to risk - or risk to live - are blessed with multiple lives!"

114

"I've never been one to take risks," said Julian.

"Yet here you are..."

"And where is here?"

"A place where we see ourselves reflected in nature - from the smallest insect to the most awesome volcano. We are in the clouds. We are patterned as the veins of each leaf. We are thinking cells. We are waves and light and weather. We are memories of variation. We live within a split second. Our feelings color in life's outline, and thus we put our own peculiar charge upon existence."

"I would never have dared to wish for this," said Julian.

"*Ah*," quoted Amie, "*but a man's reach should exceed his grasp, or what's a Heaven for?*"

Back at Amie's tree house, Julian graciously received the gift of the foot-and-a-half diameter tortoise shell. In return he presented Amie with the hand-tied fishing lures. She stored the charms with her homemade jewelry rather than with her nets and poles, then earnestly involved herself in the creation of *Chelonia* stew. It would simmer all day long in a stone cauldron over glowing coals.

It was a warm morning and Julian lolled shirtless and barefoot. He nibbled on wild raspberries and watched Amie at work, though he could not seem to dismiss the image of his reflection as it had appeared to him in the bathing pool. Even though his blond beard had grown full, there was no mistaking that facial ridges and furrows, once so familiar, had disappeared. He observed that the skin on his hands now felt supple, more pliant. Weathered creases had receded; bony ridges appeared tapered to perfect symmetry. The muscles in his forearms, once weak and pathetic, had become tough and sinewy.

"Your shoes are falling apart," Amie observed.

"Nowadays everything is made in foreign markets," Julian lamented absently. "Cheap labor. Poor quality..."

Amie looked at him curiously. Chopping wild onions to season reptilian flesh, she said, "Tonight I will make you a pair of sandals."

"I suppose I could use them," said Julian. "The skin on my feet is dry and cracking."

"It's the salt water," said Amie. "And the hot sand... But I have something for that, too."

"You know, it's really not so bad here," Julian allowed.

Less inclined to give herself away, Amie instead chose to question him about the circumstances surrounding his arrival on the island, and about his recently surrendered life in civilization. Julian related the saga of his impromptu trip to Hawaii, and how he'd spontaneously bought the Scoundrel from Kamehaloha Kong. He told her about the trip to Hilo with Kamehaloha and Tamara to watch the landing of *Hawai'iloa*, about BV's adoption, and about his breakdown off the Kona Coast. Several weeks adrift, followed by a vertiginous storm, had brought him to this disregarded atoll.

"Do you have a family?" she asked.

"I was married almost twenty years," he related. "But we divorced several years ago. I do have a daughter, though I have not seen her since she moved to Seattle."

"Then you were living alone..."

"For the past few years," he confirmed.

"Did you love your wife?" Amie asked.

Julian found the question peculiar, and a little invasive. "Why do you ask?"

"I was married once," Amie offered.

"Before you came here, of course."

"Yes..."

"So your husband was not with you when -"

"When I was marooned here," she finished.

"Why were you sailing the Pacific alone?" Julian inquired.

"After several record-breaking voyages, I needed one last effort to ensure my reputation, so I decided to make an all-out effort to go around the world. An empirical challenge... A fool's play, as it turned out."

"I do not recall hearing about your voyage," said Julian.

"Oh, it was in the press all right!"

"Your husband must have been devastated when he realized you were lost," said Julian.

"I was very important to him, though I suspect not in a romantic way," said Amie. She placed the chopped scallions into the cooking pot with the meat and tubers.

"But he must have mobilized a search for you..."

"I'm sure he did."

"Then perhaps there's still hope we will be found!" said Julian.

"Not by *his* efforts," Amie said matter-of-factly.

"Why not?" Julian asked.

"I'm sure my husband is deceased now," said Amie.

"But how could you know that?"

"It's been a long time," she said.

"How old *are* you?" Julian asked.

Amie ran slender fingers through her long hair, took a deep breath, then sighed. A very queer expression settled over her features. "In truth, I don't know anymore. I stopped counting in days and months and years. But that doesn't matter," she said. "Time is different here."

"So you keep telling me."

"I'm not surprised you don't understand. But soon you will."

"Here, it seems, we have nothing *but* time," said Julian.

"Precisely," said Amie.

Amie took Julian and Buenaventura to the place she called Turtle Cove. Soon, Jewel joined them. The two parrots perched together on a nearby hydrangea limb. They talked in low tones, preened one another, and observed the humans with great curiosity.

As usual the sea turtles were bobbing in swells and surf. Julian and Amie moved onto a large rock for a better vantage point. It was fun watching the turtles submerge themselves, then trying to guess where they might surface for air.

"People wish for all kinds of things," Julian conjectured, "but seldom do they imagine that their wishes might somehow come true."

"Before I came here," Amie confided, "my life was filled with demands and expectations - not all of my creation!"

"Your husband?" Julian inquired.

"Yes... And others, too. I was constantly wishing for peace and solitude."

"I guess you got your wish."

"Perhaps there are no accidents," Amie speculated. "What if events and situations manifest out of our deepest feelings and desires? What if the universe operates on a causative dynamic, taking us always at our word and fabricating each and every situation from our own fantasies? It's occurred to me, Julian, that I was marooned here by my own desire for retreat."

"But why would anybody wish to be stranded without hope?" he asked.

"Even before I left on my around-the-world trip, I felt as though I had accomplished everything relevant to the life I was living. I knew the possibility existed that I wouldn't make it home. On a deeper level, perhaps I was even hoping that some twist of fate would lead me painlessly into eternity. That almost happened."

"But you're so vivacious! I can't imagine you actually wanting to die."

"Well, I never thought about it in terms of mortality. But I did speculate endlessly about being swallowed by the sea."

"Sounds morbid," said Julian.

"It never seemed so to me."

"What about your husband?" Julian probed. "And what about others you loved? Or those who loved you?"

"I never realized it before I was lost - at least not consciously - but after all this time alone, I'm sure I've never really loved anybody. And I doubt anyone ever loved me!"

As a long shadow moved over the shoreline a breeze came up suddenly out of the northeast. Leaves rustled, a flower petal dropped, the humming of the forest insects abruptly ceased.

"What was it like for you once you knew you were lost?"

"It felt inevitable," said Amie. "I remember there was only sea and sky, spinning and spinning, and finally merging.

After a while I was no longer able to distinguish the horizon. I could have sailed over the edge of existence, or sunk like a hulk to the bottom of the ocean. I could have flown straight into the sun, like foolish Icarus. For I had dreams - ambitious dreams! I was the one who was always pushing limits - not only for myself, but for causes bigger than any individual!"

"Yet in the midst of all your aspirations, there was a voice calling out for rest and solitude," said Julian. "So you subconsciously struck a bargain with fate to be marooned on this deserted island..."

"I suppose I've always needed an impossible challenge," Amie assessed. "There were others who wanted me. Men of asinine courage. Some of them didn't even like me - like Freddy."

"Somebody you loved?"

Amie shrugged. "Maybe in my more self-destructive moods," she conjectured. "We were in Burma together. We rode elephants in Thailand. Can you imagine?"

Though he might never have envisioned himself eating and enjoying reptilian meat, the evening meal of turtle stew offered a delightful change for Julian's wearied taste buds. Savoring each spoonful of the unorthodox ragout, he requested more broth once he had eaten the gist. They drank tea made from raspberry leaves. After finishing the main course, they nibbled on dried bits of coconut and wedges of breadfruit.

Darkness came, and before Amie lit the torches the Pleiades were visible in the northern sky. Tireless in her ministrations, she rubbed oil on Julian's cracked and blistered feet. She knew the oil would soften hardened skin and promote healing. When she finished she measured his feet for the promised sandals, then wrapped them in a warm compress.

"You're very kind," Julian thanked her.

"If you form ulcers on your feet, they could become infected. There's no sulfa here."

"Have you been ill since arriving here?" Julian asked.

"Only once," said Amie. "But it was a sickness of the heart."

The admission seemed so personal that Julian chose not to inquire further. No doubt there was much to learn about the beautiful and enigmatic Amie. Some indeterminate power had cast them in this isolated drama. The elements served as backdrop; the sea and sky were dreams. The islet was a finite landscape, but the terrain of the soul was immeasurable.

That night they slept not together, yet near enough to whisper recollections and acknowledgments of hope. Julian lay on his back and quietly pondered the depth of a less than familiar sky. He listened to her measured breaths and felt the radiant warmth of her body from a distance as Amie fell asleep first.

Next morning Amie urged Julian to return to his own home. She genuinely appreciated his company, she explained sweetly, but she needed time to adjust to the fact that she was no longer alone on the island. Reluctantly he obeyed her request. He was sure there would be other nights.

With his tortoise shell basin strapped on his back and walking in newly fashioned sandals, he hiked round the steamy, verdant cove. He stopped to taste the dew that had collected on the petals of an orchid. He marveled at the two-foot-diameter, gossamer web spun by a sinister-looking spider. And as he reached the pinnacle of the promontory, he caught sight of the Scoundrel, disabled and helpless and bobbing in the surf that spread across the reef.

At present Amie chose not to share her routines, and Buenaventura, too, declined to fraternize with Julian this morning. Presumably BV had departed with his steadfast mate, Jewel. Again Julian found himself a solitary cast upon a lonely shore, and he marched up and down the beach trying to codify an impossible situation.

The sun shone through dense haze and the temperature continued to climb. This morning the Trades were not blowing. The humidity became oppressive. Julian tried retreating to a shady notch, but swarms of gnats finally drove him back onto the sun-soaked beach. He stripped off his shirt and stored his sandals. Then he cut off his pant legs with the dull blade of his

120

pocket knife. He tied back his scruffy hair with a piece of twine. He wrapped his head in a saturated T-shirt. But generally such efforts contributed little to his comfort.

Bathing his frying feet in the surf, Julian noticed a curious object floating amidst the foam about thirty feet out to sea. He waded into the surf to have a closer look. It seemed to be a bottle. Motivated mostly by the possibility that he might make use of the jar, he retrieved the vessel.

Clutching the carafe in his hand, Julian waded all the way back to shore before he noticed the scrap of paper sealed inside the receptacle. Standing barefoot on the sand where surf met shore, he unscrewed the bottle cap to get at the piece of paper. Once he had pulled the note through the bottleneck and over the mouth and looked at the vaguely familiar handwriting, he felt himself swept up in a wave of synchronicity. The message read:

"Wili-Wili come.
Make ready!
- Kong"

A sour expression spread across Julian's face as he visualized Kong's ironic smile. "You probably think this is funny, Kamehaloha," Julian yelled. "But I am not amused!" He tore up the note into tiny pieces and flung it back into the ocean.

"An egg is one bird's way of becoming other eggs," said Jewel to Buenaventura.

"Are you trying to tell me I am going to be a father?"

"If you are true to your name..."

During the time since Jewel's arrival their sense of mutual destiny had grown stronger with each shared experience. They soared together above precipice and coastline, played spirited games in the dense and wonderful rain forest, then took refuge each night in the protected recess of their tree hollow. And they had become aware of other islands nearby - virtually hundreds of life-sustaining land masses within a circumference quite reachable by unbroken flight. One by one, they meant to

121

visit each tiny atoll, establishing a colonial legacy within this particular region of the Pacific.

Now the two parrots made a cozy nest in the hollowed-out trunk of a pili nut tree, and there Jewel brooded over her eggs. It would take twenty days for the eight chicks to hatch. During that time it was Buenaventura's role to protect Jewel and bring her food - a duty he undertook with single-minded fealty.

Amie started the day cultivating the soil between rows of sweet potatoes, but as the heat and humidity began to build she threw down her hoe and abandoned the weeding project. Wiping away sticky perspiration from her forehead and face, she sat upon the red earth and quenched her thirst with a cupful of water brought from her cistern.

In the privacy of her garden she thought about Julian's recently finished home on the beach front and realized that he must now be sweltering. Since his arrival the Trades had been blowing without a break. This was his first real experience with the tropical heat. Amie certainly could have invited him back to her encampment to bathe with her in the cool waters of the Seven Sisters, but she was presently experiencing some hesitancy when it came to furthering their fledgling relationship. Indeed, how could she even consider sharing the most intimate aspects of her life with another man? Even her marriage to G.P. was predicated upon the condition that if, after one year's time, she were not happy with the marriage, he would release her from her commitment, no questions asked. For various reasons, the least of which being love, she had never exercised that option.

"It's insane not to put a radar beacon on Howland," she'd protested repeatedly as they planned the around-the-world voyage together.

"But we're critically over budget," he intoned. "Besides, the *Itasca* will be nearby, and Fred Noonan is the best navigator in the business."

"When he's not drunk or hung over," she said.

"Take a trailing wire instead," he told her.

"I have never once taken a trailing wire."

"You'll have no trouble finding Howland," G.P. assured her. "Why worry? You've been flawless in the past." He put his arm around her, as if at this point such a gesture might provide consolation. "Once this trip is over, and you're back home safe and sound, you'll be a national hero - an icon! You can rest for a couple of weeks, then there'll be ticker tape parades and speaking engagements and probably even a dinner at the White House!"

"I'm not sure I want Freddy Noonan along on this trip, G.P."

"There's nobody else," he said sternly. "Besides, it's all arranged. We can't be changing things now or we'll go belly-up. Dead broke. No more flights. No more anything. You don't want that, my love..."

She turned her back on him and walked away in disgust. There would be no beacon put on Howland, but she would make the flight anyway - perhaps as much to spite G.P. as for any other reason. And she would make Freddy pledge not to drink during this expedition...

In the end she knew there were deeper reasons she had not stuck to her guns and insisted that a radar beacon be placed on Howland Island. Flying around the world - even in a plane as worthy as the *Electra* - was not without considerable risk. Without luck they might be lost before they reached Africa! Though she never really believed that... More likely, if they were to disappear, it would be somewhere over the vast waters of the Pacific. And she had been fascinated with the prospect of peace in oblivion.

Of course that was before she'd come to know the inherent sweetness of this natural oasis. Now death seemed far away indeed. Unfortunately, Freddy had not survived to share this new perspective.

Julian was another matter altogether. He seemed to be a different type of man - much less inclined to try to dominate her. Right from the start Amie sensed a comic ineptness about him - not that he was helpless, but he lacked the bravado so characteristic of other men she had known. Admittedly, she found

Julian's naiveté rather endearing, and Amie cautioned herself against affection out of sympathy.

"Did I actually receive a message in a bottle from Kong?" Julian wondered aloud. "By what means could such a thing have happened?"

The vessel lay cast aside on the sand, but of course no evidence remained of the cryptic note. Julian slumped on the shore to ponder the anomaly. Gnats gathered round his head, drawn by the sweat pouring off his tomato-ripe face.

Confounded to the point of self-doubt, he got to his feet and tramped over to his shelter. Rifling through his effects, he found the quill Amie had given him and began scrawling a reply to Kong's warning upon a piece of paper bark.

"Kamehaloha -

You once said we had mutual business. I thought you were referring to me buying the Scoundrel. Now I'm stranded here. Is this your doing? Don't get me wrong: the island is nice. But this isn't fair. I am a simple man. I just wanted a vacation after being fired. If you and your friends possess some sort of weird power, I would rather you play your games with somebody else. This is not my idea of a joke!
                              Julian"

He rolled his finished note into a scroll, then walked across the sand to collect the errant bottle. Stuffing his reply inside the jar, he flung it as far as he could into the surf. The bottle came down just beyond the reef, and Julian stood watching it. Within minutes the jar washed back on shore. Apparently the conduit on which Kong's message had arrived was not working in both directions.

"I must be going insane," Julian muttered as he stared out to sea. "And that would be worse than death. Because now I believe I have received a taunting message in a bottle from half way across the Pacific. If that's not enough, I'm trying to send a response! I find myself conversing with parrots. I'm eating

124

leaves and grasses. And I've found a siren on an otherwise deserted tropical island. Get hold of yourself! This is pure dream stuff. I should pinch myself awake and be done with this foolishness. But there floats the Scoundrel, chained to the reef. The carbs choke at my touch. What am I to do? Amie is incredibly beautiful..."

# PART III.

Chapter 1.

     With ill-concealed anxiety, George Putnam paced the floor at coast guard headquarters in San Francisco. Tiny beads of sweat formed on his high forehead, while dark circles outlined sleepless eyes. With the cuffs of his white shirt turned up to mid-forearm, its once-stiff collar lay open. Along with pretense and decorum, he'd discarded his tie hours ago. For twenty hours G.P. had stepped off his apprehension in nervous strides, wishing only that the night would be over and the crossing completed. When first news came from *Itasca*, he could not believe what he was reading:

     "EARHART CONTACT 0742 REPORTED ONE HALF HOUR FUEL AND NO LANDFALL. POSITION DOUBTFUL. CONTACT 0646 REPORTED ONE HUNDRED MILES FROM ITASCA BUT NO RELATIVE BEARING. 0843 REPORTED LINE OF POSITION 157 DASH 337 BUT NO REFERENCE POINT PRESUME HOWLAND. ESTIMATE 1200 FOR MAXIMUM TIME ALOFT AND IF NON-ARRIVAL BY THAT TIME WILL COMMENCE SEARCH IN NORTHWEST QUADRANT FROM HOWLAND AS MOST PROBABLE AREA... UNDERSTAND SHE WILL FLOAT FOR LIMITED TIME."

126

"Yes, the plane should float," G.P. told an attentive *Herald Tribune* reporter who had kept vigil with him all night long. "But of course I cannot estimate for how long. Remember, a Lockheed plane has never been forced down at sea before. The plane's large wing span and empty fuel tanks will provide sufficient buoyancy, that is, if it comes to rest on the sea without being damaged. And don't forget that there is a two-man life raft aboard. Also, life belts, flares, a Very pistol, and a large yellow signal kite."

G.P. could hardly fathom the news he was receiving, sparse though it was. Nor could he believe his baleful prevision. More likely, he expected word to come at any moment of their discovery, either on some obscure island or ditched at sea. He expected to hear that each was safe. Countless times he'd waited on pins and needles for word to come of his wife's safe landing, and while there had been any number of perilous moments, Amelia had never disappointed - neither him nor her adoring public. Knowing this was to be her last venture flight, G.P. proscribed the irony that catastrophe might befall her now.

A young radio operator informed George that he had personally read a dispatch from Captain Thompson of the *Itasca* requesting the assistance of a PBY flying boat. Dispatched with a crew of eight from Honolulu, the craft was to aid the search in the vicinity of Howland Island. The prevailing weather between the Hawaiian Islands and the Marshall Islands was questionable, though, and it was unclear if the PBY would be able to take part immediately in the search. G.P. graciously thanked the radio technician for the information then went to find a telephone. He had several calls to make.

The first call he placed was to Amelia's mother, Amy Otis Earhart. George knew she would be waiting for word of Amelia's triumph. How could he tell her that her daughter was missing over the Pacific? His voice quivered out of control. Nevertheless, he tried to remain positive as he spoke.

"Mother Earhart, this is George..."

"Where are you, George?" implored Amy Earhart.

"I'm in San Francisco, at coast guard headquarters. Have you heard the news yet?"

"It's all over the radio, George," said Amy. Considering the circumstance, she sounded surprisingly calm.

"I don't want you to worry, Mother Earhart. Everything possible is being done to find Amelia. This is not the time to think the worst."

"Amelia is *not* dead, George," said Amy matter-of-factly. "I'm quite certain of that."

"Of course not..." He seemed to be reassuring himself as much as giving comfort to his mother-in-law.

Amelia's mother took charge of the conversation: "Weeks before she left on this flight, Amelia said there were certain things she could not tell me. At the time I thought she was being cryptic for the sake of drama, but now it all makes sense to me. I'm convinced this has something to do with those visits to the White House, George. You must urge Roosevelt to tell us everything he knows!"

"Mother Earhart, he's the President of the United States! What can I say to him?"

"Whatever is necessary, George... I'm certain he knows what's happened to her. And I know she's alive, George. I feel it in my bones."

The son-in-law promised to call the White House.

G.P.'s next call was to Jackie Cochran, Amelia's long time friend and psychic consultant. Personally, G.P. doubted her abilities, but he was desperate for any information whatsoever. "Anything you can tell me, Jackie," he implored, "might save Amelia's life!"

Of course Jackie Cochran wanted to help Amelia, but her consent held conditions. "I'll share my impressions, George, but you must promise to keep my name out of the papers. Not one word to the press!"

"You have my word, Jackie."

The psychic began, "I was aware immediately that Amelia was in peril. She came down quite unexpectedly... On a deserted island south and east of her intended landing site. She's

128

quite disoriented, but definitely alive! Exact location of the island is uncertain, I'm afraid..."

"Is she hurt?" he wanted to know.

"She has only minor injuries, though Mr. Noonan fractured his skull on a bulkhead. He didn't make it, I'm afraid. I'm terribly sorry, George."

"Anything more?" G.P. solicited.

"There is a boat called the *Itasca* nearby. . Also, there is a Japanese fishing vessel in the vicinity. But, search as they may, neither will locate this island."

"Why not?" G.P. asked.

"This is very, very strange," Jackie noted. "While they are apparently searching for her in the right *place*, they *seem to* be in the wrong *time*..."

"I don't understand, Jackie," said G.P.

"Nor do I," said the psychic. "And neither will anyone else. This mystery will persist until the nature of time itself is clear to everyone."

To say the least, G.P. felt spooked by the psychic's discarnate forecast, though he wasted no time requesting that a search be initiated for an obscure island southeast of Howland in the Phoenix group. Close contacts at navy headquarters accommodated him without delay, and the U.S.S. *Colorado* made full steam to the locality in question. The ship's captain sent up all three of his 3U-3 spotter planes, but each pilot reported that he could not even locate the reefs and atolls for which he searched.

Nevertheless, the *Colorado* continued searching, visiting Enderbury, Phoenix, McKean, Gardner, and Hull Island. Only Hull was inhabited, but the islanders had never even heard of Amelia Earhart.

Besides visual search efforts, radio massages were broadcast repeatedly, a simple hail devised by G.P. himself: "*AE - Land or water? North or south?*"

Coast guard navigators prepared, at G.P.'s insistence, a chart of the great circle 'base course' from Lea, New Guinea to Howland Island. Putnam assumed Noonan would have attempted to calculate a drift angle as soon after take-off as possible. From

129

...able weather reports G.P. was able to predict their possible drift to be plus or minus eleven degrees. Projecting this track across the breadth of the south Pacific, he surmised they might have passed as much as one hundred forty miles south of Howland. That course concurred with Jackie Cochran's vision. And there remained the enigmatic conundrum proposed by the psychic concerning a fundamental discrepancy in time itself! Yet it was also possible that exactly the opposite drift ratio had occurred, putting Amelia and Fred one hundred forty miles north of their target, down somewhere in the outlying islands of the Marshalls. G.P. knew that each atoll would have to be searched.

All the while Putnam never stopped talking to the reporters who gathered at coast guard headquarters in San Francisco. "AE will pull through," he told a writer from the New York *Sunday Mirror.* "Of course I'm worried, but she has more courage than anyone I know. And I have confidence in her ability to handle any situation. She's likely to turn up with hardly a hair out of place. That's AE!"

While G.P. was talking to the reporters the radio operator who had kept him informed over the course of two days passed him a transcription of a communiqué from the PBY flying boat:

"LAST TWO HOURS IN EXTREMELY BAD WEATHER BETWEEN ALTITUDE 2000 AND 12000 FEET. SNOW, SLEET, RAIN, ELECTRICAL STORMS. IN DAYLIGHT CONDITIONS LOOK EQUALLY BAD. CLOUD TOPS APPEAR TO BE 18000 FEET OR MORE. RETURNING TO PEARL HARBOR."

By now Vidal had arrived from Washington. Going head to head with G.P., he had his own ideas concerning the parameters of the search. Hardly the best of friends, the two men here had a common cause - Amelia's rescue and well-being. They found a quiet corner out of earshot where reporters would not disturb them.

"Look!" said Gene. "They're out there trying to cover three million square miles. Obviously that's an impossible task. The search *must* be narrowed."

"Narrowed to where?" Putnam wanted to know.

"Before the flight," said Gene, "she told me that if I could not locate Howland she would probably turn back toward the Marshalls. It's there we must concentrate our effort!"

"Can we get help from high office?" Putnam asked.

"What exactly do you mean, George?"

"I mean from FDR?"

"I don't have a direct line to the president," said Vidal.

"What about the DOC? They built the runway!"

"Yes, I'm sure I can count on the secretary," said Vidal.

Putnam nodded. Acknowledging Vidal's influence, George began to trust that someone in a lofty position would spearhead a concerted search and rescue effort. He implored Vidal to cable the Secretary of Commerce at once.

"...REQUEST YOUR GOOD OFFICES IN OBTAINING COOPERATION OF BRITISH AND JAPANESE IN CONTINUING SEARCH ESPECIALLY REGARDING ELLICE, GILBERT, AND MARSHALL ISLANDS, OCEAN ISLAND AND AREA NORTHEAST OF SAME. ALSO IF POSSIBLE REQUEST SOME EXAMINATION OF ISLAND NORTHERLY AND NORTHWESTERLY OF PAGO PAGO. CONFIDENTIAL INFORMATION: EXTRAORDINARY EVIDENCE SEEMS TO EXIST INDICATING CASTAWAY STILL LIVING, THOUGH OF SUCH STRANGE NATURE CANNOT BE OFFICIAL OR PUBLICLY CONFIRMED."

"If we're narrowing the search," George inquired, "why the Gilberts? We're talking about sixteen coral reefs located six hundred miles west of Howland - a mere two hundred square miles of land scattered haphazardly over more than a million square miles of ocean!"

"Consider the titanic ocean current," said Vidal. "It swirls westward along the equator in that area. The drift, aided by constant trade winds, could possibly carry a floating object westward for a significant distance."

So with the impetus of Washington the search continued. Unprecedented, the cost of such an operation mounted steadily, past four million dollars. President Roosevelt took some heat for the expenditure on behalf of a private citizen, but he was able to

131

off his detractors, stating that the ships and personnel would have been engaged anyway, and that the search enabled the navy to survey areas which were previously not well-charted and were now under Japanese control. Deeply concerned for the welfare of the young, female flying ace, the president publicly expressed his solicitude. And in her weekly newspaper column Eleanor Roosevelt also voiced her regard for Amelia: "I feel that if she comes through safely she will feel that what she has learned makes it all worthwhile. But her friends will wish that service could be rendered without such risk to a person whom many love..."

By the end of July, the *official* search was called off. Still, George was unwilling to give up hope. From Washington he told Amy, "Opinion seems unanimous that Amelia is somehow, somewhere, still alive. We are doing everything possible to find her."

Chapter 2.

For five days the trade winds had not come. The cruel heat would not relent, and the humidity wrapped round the island like liquid amber. Pestered by biting flies and swarms of gnats even at midnight, Julian lay, naked, on his hammock, fanning himself with a frond. The air remained motionless and stifling.

Waking to leaden skies he decided to hike over the divide to look for Amie where the great waterfall plunged endlessly into the Seven Sisters. There they might languish in the cool water to allay their torrid misery.

Her endurance tested by oppressive weather, Amie welcomed him as a friend, and together they bathed in the restorative waters. In her hair Amie wore a brilliant red blossom; around her neck, a plumeria lei.

The compelling glow upon her cheeks made Amie's face seem like a floral corolla. Amidst many splendors, Julian saw Amie as the most beautiful woman he'd ever laid eyes upon. Helplessly enamored, he was left breathless and reeling. Julian did not want to take his eyes off her. Not ever!

Afflicted and depleted on the beach, Julian had seemed almost pathetic to Amie at first, but now, as she washed his shaggy hair and trickled clear water over his face with her fingers, knowledged the obvious change in his physical bearing. e rejuvenating reservoir was working its magic on him, just as t had, over time, on her.

Now convinced that she did not want him gone, the very idea of being cast again into suffocating loneliness seemed a desolation Amie could not endure, yet her sentiments for Julian had outpaced mere need. She had begun to experience feelings of unabashed desire for the man. For Amie, such empathy had been long suppressed - not only since being marooned on the island, but perhaps before that.

"What relief!" Julian proclaimed as he submerged himself in the cool, fresh water, then came up sputtering.

"I don't mind the heat," said Amie, "but the humidity is unbearable."

"Is it like this often?" Julian asked.

"Only when the Trades don't blow."

"It's miserable out of the water."

"I know a place where it's much cooler," said Amie. "It's quite far, though. And it's a difficult ascent. There's a cave near the cinder cone where we can sleep."

"I'm up for the climb," said Julian. "What do we need to bring?"

"Very little... A basket of fruit. A tapa cloth on which to lie. Nothing more."

Walking over a narrow trail, just behind Amie, Julian moved along sheer cliffs which in places dropped hundreds of feet to the ocean. Venturing deeper into these primitive hanging valleys than he had yet gone, Julian was amazed by the wild profusion of flowers. Ginger and ti formed the understory in forests of kukui, mango, and bamboo. Pandanus abounded along the rugged and precarious coastal cliffs. And as they neared the cone-studded, volcanic crater, streaks of yellow, gray, and black traced the courses of ancient lava flows. Pictographs painted by long-forgotten artists were carved upon stone walls.

"This place is called *Po*," Amie informed Julian. "Do not ask me how I know this: I simply know it. *Po* is an ocean of

134

time. It is eternity. A place where sea, sky, and land become one."

"You're trying to frighten the hell out of me," Julian conferred.

Having nearly forgotten the emotion herself, Amie was surprised by his allusion to fear. "When I landed here," she told him, "I thought I was ready for death. But I did not die. In fact, as you've seen, Julian, there's a regenerative force present in this place that defies explanation." She sat near to him on a stone and offered him water from her salvaged canteen. "Now I often dream about my own death - though I question if death even exists here. Perhaps the most cruel tragedy of all would be to wander forever over strand and through forest, homeless and hungry to the point of craving, an intruder in Heaven, welcome nowhere."

At the volcano's summit, looking over steep, variegated escarpments, and finally to the shore where the open sea boomed upon carpets of untrodden sand, Julian vicariously felt the pulse of the earth throbbing within his veins.    Understanding the reverence he felt for term and creation, Amie took Julian by the hand and led him over the warm loam to the mouth of a cave once consigned to ceremony - or perhaps sanctioned as a sepulcher. Smooth and dusky stones, slippery with moisture, shone in the pale light, and soft, green moss framed the cavern's aperture. Though she spoke softly, her voice echoed within the recess.

"We experience ourselves as fevered, dancing electrons, revolving in this fanciful orbit or that, barely acknowledging the nucleus we circle..."

His hand tightened within hers, and she noticed in his grasp a slight trembling.   She was moved by his trust. With dream-like improbability, a geological fault had opened in the ground upon which they'd been treading. Suddenly they seemed enfolded within an incalculable moment - a segment beyond all apogee - one that might be shared only by complementaries. Amie considered how uncommon it was to find one of compatible disposition. Their eyes met in a headlong glance of affection.

Inside the burrow they felt the respite of a subterranean sanctuary. This retreat, with its mysterious, shadowy niches, and images of half-seen forms, challenged perception to move beyond the customary margins of the senses, and into more empirical realms of understanding. Abandoned or lost, they had discovered one another within the very pitch of remoteness, and for Julian the flesh he had not touched in love was now radiant in proximity. He offered the brush of his fingertips to bridge remaining distance and calm apprehension.

And while barely perceptible, internal currents warned Amie of something both imminent and profound, she was neither afraid nor resistant. Though the egotism and impatience of other men pulled at her memory, she acknowledged that Julian - though perhaps graceless at other endeavors - was nonetheless a gallant suitor.

Amie moved closer to better feel his presence. His skin gave off the scent of freshly milled koa wood. His hair was dressed with an herbal potpourri of her making. Amie embraced the luxury of abandonment as rings of thunder moved through valleys and over mountain tops, gathering its energy round their refuge. Outside, the drops began to lightly fall.

Moving to the mouth of the cave she stared at the rain. Inevitably it came after a humid interval. Experiencing an ecstatic desire to go rushing into the shower, she pulled off her halter and unfastened her skirt. Spreading her arms, Amie ran, naked, from the cave into the mist.

Julian rushed to the opening to see her frolic in the sprinkle. Her figure was lithe; wetness glistened upon her shoulders and back. Without qualm, Julian shed his clothing and went running in her footsteps. Over coarse volcanic ground he moved, into the dense and humid forest. What exhilaration! Ahead he could see Amie's angular body moving swiftly through the dripping boughs - a mercurial animal in flight. Once Julian might have been breathless in pursuit, but now he was practically equal to her agility. Overtaking her in a field of ferns, he reached out and encircled her bare waist with his well-muscled arm. Amie's rain-soaked hair was plastered over her forehead and face,

and her lips glimmered. She *needed to pull her close.* She
playfully, resisted half-hearted, *then* laughed. The
continued drenching them, and *Amie shivered* slightly in th
uncharacteristic embrace of his and *Boldly,* Julian strung
nearly imperceptible kisses, like the beads *of a necklace,* round
her throat.

Trying at once to lift the mantle of *little remembered*
sensations, Amie was out of synch with each *overture. Julian*
moved to kiss her lips. She did not resist. His *breath smelled of*
mint and his tongue went round and round inside *her mouth,*
stopping finally for a single touch upon the tip of her *upper lip.*
The sparks of an erupting volcano ignited long-forgotten passions
as he ran his open palms over her thighs and legs, as if he were
sculpting her out of clay!

They fell together among soft ferns. Slippery with rain
water, their bodies were cool yet burning. The heat of his parched
lips passed to hers. His tongue explored the recess behind her
small earlobes. Her skin tasted sweet, like dampened flower
petals. Amie's body rolled like the waves of the great ocean and
she did not close her eyes until they lay, rain soaked, in the
afterglow of fulfillment. Amie realized she would never again
hear the sound of rain without remembering these first intimate
moments with the castaway.

Back inside the ancient cave Julian watched in fascination
as she dried herself with the tapa.

"The paragon we find in love is at once common and
improbable," she told him. "We pass untold days shrouded in
slumberous silence, constructing moments of blissful union. And
we sustain ourselves in spite of insularity, waiting and waiting for
the divine touch of a stranger."

Julian was nearly overcome with the power of her voice.
He moved toward her. Amidst deepening folds of the earth's
cavern, he kissed her lightly. The cave's lichen-covered walls
seemed to whisper words of encouragement, audible not by
human ears, but by the auricle of the soul. Amie moved again to
the mouth of the grotto and looked outside. "The rain is letting up
now," she said.

137

...ulian, too, scanned the perimeter of the ___ "But the ___ is not yet finished," he said.

Together they ate the fruit Amie had ___ with her, and in late afternoon they lay together again, ___ with the power of an tapa-covered stone. Julian made love ___ feelings of urgency and effaced god - a god resurrected by ___ passion. Nearing climax, Julian envisioned the fire of the once terrible volcano. He called out her name repeatedly, like a disincarnate spirit. "Amie, Amie, Amie..."

And as the resounding thunder came again, she was lost to the increments of her history. Reverie slowly slipped away, and Amie arose and went to the opening to assess the storm that was gathering power.

The sky was black and portentous. Fog hung low in the valleys. She could see that the ocean had changed from its normally placid shade of blue to an ominous cast of steely gray. White-capped waves grew wrathful as they came pounding over reef and shore. No doubt they were lucky to have the protection of the cave, but unless the storm passed quickly, they would be sequestered.

"It looks like we're in for a very bad time," she told Julian.

"As the rain falls outside, we'll make love all night long," he ventured.

"You don't understand," she said. "The wind could reach gale force. The storm surge might advance three hundred yards inland. It's a good thing we came here, Julian. This is Wili-Wili!"

He turned quickly at her exclamation. "What did you call it?" he demanded.

"Wili-Wili - a powerful typhoon," she defined.

"Kong said it would come," he muttered. "But how could he have known?" Julian felt somehow manipulated by his curious Hawaiian acquaintances. He spat in frustration as the understanding of an enigma so meddlesome yet eluded him. "What about our homes and supplies?" he asked. "How can we protect them?"

138

"It's too late," said Arnie. "We must remain far or we could be swept out to sea by the surge."

"But I must make certain the scoundrel is secure," Julian protested.

"Even now the waves are too high," Julian. "Such storms approach very fast. If you try to swim out to your boat, the curls will dash you against the reef. You would be killed."

"How long will the storm last?" he wanted to know.

"Since I came to the island, Wili-Wili has come twice before. Once it lasted only over night. The other time I was here in the cave three days and two nights. But it's the only place on the island where I know we will be safe."

"There's nothing for us to eat," he observed.

"I will go down the mountain, to the groves, and gather food for us," she said.

"I'll go with you," he presumed.

"No, you'll only slow me down. I know every step of the trail - every turn, every rock."

"But can you carry enough fruit to last out the storm?"

Her heuristic expression chagrined him somewhat. "By now," she said, "I would have thought you'd believe in me..." She prepared to journey down the mountainside.

Julian stood at the mouth of the cave and watched as she started across the cinder cone, the expression of one well acquainted with risky endeavors and tenuous missions written upon the contours of her smooth face. He followed her path as she strode with unfaltering determination over the ridges and fissures of the lava field. In the space of a single breath, Arnie disappeared into the rain forest.

Chapter 3.

The rain, at first a welcome shower, was now a deluge. The easterly wind blew fiercely, stripping leaves from vines and bending the tops of the tall palms almost to breaking. Caught by the raging gale, pieces of leaf and bough, sand, feathers, and foam flew through the air, spun into senseless vertigo. With hand held over his brow, Julian peered across the crater where the trail opened onto the lava plain. Amie was not in sight. Through torrential sheets of rain he could scarcely distinguish the shoreline and horizon. He realized that even if Amie had managed to make it to the groves before the squall had grown to such intensity, there was little chance she would return until it ended. He hoped she had found shelter to wait out the storm.

"I should never have let her go alone," he said to himself. "The trail is steep and perilous - no doubt slippery once wet. If anything has happened to her..."

He retreated back inside the cave to escape the downpour. Sitting upon the broad stone, chin in hand, he consternated. If Amie did not return soon, he thought, he would have to look for her. But such a search posed problems. What if he, himself, became lost? Where the forest was particularly dense the trail was not always evident - especially for one who had traversed the path only once. And what if Amie had taken some alternate route? They might pass each other unaware while moving in opposite directions. That would be a disaster. Julian would simply have to trust her acumen. And wait.

He remembered the first time he'd seen her. Standing under broad leaves in the banana grove, sunlight had filtered through the canopy of fronds and shone favorably upon her face. Even then she embodied grace. Julian thought: some people take light in a special way; it penetrates their skin, illuminating them from within, then reflects itself off perfect equanimity, shining outward like a beacon. Julian was drawn, without regret, to Amie's light. Her charity, at first, had ensured his well being. Encouragement and camaraderie followed. Finally she had offered love to fill a long cultivated void in his life. Now as the storm compounded itself by the minute, he feared for her safety.

Outside the tempest raged, and Julian could not sit idly inside the cave while Amie's whereabouts and condition remained uncertain. Naked, except for shorts and his newly made sennit sandals, he stood in the pelting rain and looked out to sea. Initially he thought he was seeing through the storm's curtain to a line where angry sea met leaden sky, but as he continued to look at the pitching water he realized that what he was actually seeing was not the horizon at all, but a thunderous wall of water perhaps thirty feet high and still several miles beyond the reef. Of course it was curling its way toward shore.

"Oh, my God!" he gasped. If Amie had taken shelter anywhere near the beach, she would surely be pounded, submerged, and swept out to sea.

He wiped water from his brow and face as he thought about Buenaventura. Where was his friend? And how was he faring in this war of the elements?

Debris swirled in every direction, and Julian could hear the desperate sound of cracking bark and tearing stalk. The intonation of the roaring wind reverberated through abstract canyons of improbability, touching both memory and emotion, and compromising his rationality. Not long ago this pretty little isle, drifting at the outskirts of forever, had offered security from a very different kind of storm. Now furious-looking clouds churned round and round the sanctuary, threatening to engulf all within their reach. Sublime harmony had been transformed into chaos. Julian felt the island's pain in a highly personal way, for he had come to understand that this isolated atoll had a life of its own.

Into the cutting wind Julian moved with great difficulty. The gale blew so fiercely against his face and through his long hair that he was afraid his locks might be stripped from his scalp. At last he reached the place where the lava field gave way to a forest of ravaged vegetation. He found the trail head. Nearly blown off his feet, he clutched a branch as he called with all his might for Amie. The wind stole his words before they had left his lips. Again he looked out to sea. The ominous wall of water loomed closer to shore. The surge would soon be upon them.

Left no choice, he started down the mountainside in search of Amie. Maybe she, too, had seen the massive wave and started her ascent to safety. Perhaps they would meet on the trail before landslides carried the already insecure spoor downhill and into the sea.

The red earth beneath Julian's feet was sodden. His sandals sank into thick mud; his advance was precarious and slow. Grasping the outgrowths of roots and clutching onto rocks and bare branches, he made his way in pouring rain down the side of the volcano.

At the edge of a fog-covered, dizzying cliff, he struggled with uncertain footing. One careful step after another made his distance. But just when he was feeling as though he might have gone beyond the worst part of the descent, the saturated ground and loose stones gave way underfoot and sent him repelling down a turbid slope. He clung first to one overhanging limb, which snapped under his weight, then another, which broke his fall. Julian climbed back to safety, soaked and covered head to toe in mud, and feeling fortunate to be alive.

Around a prominent arc Julian caught sight of the turbulent sea. The deadly wall of water was nearly upon them now, and he realized there was virtually no chance he would reach

Amie before the wave crashed onshore. If she were stranded within a quarter mile of the shoreline, only a miracle would save her.

Julian held his breath and watched from a ridge as the surge pounded violently over the shore. All the land near Amie's home, including her fish hatchery, her fields, and life-sustaining groves of fruit - all the way inland to the point where the towering waterfall flowed into the Seven Sisters - lay engulfed in sea water. Trees snapped like match sticks and were washed out to sea as the virulent wave receded. No doubt Amie's fine house was in ruin - if it had survived at all! And what about the Scoundrel? Julian could not imagine there might be anything left of his boat...

Once the storm surge had broken onshore the wind grew even stronger. Julian had no choice but to retreat. It took him two hours to retrace his steps, and finally reaching the sanctuary, he staggered inside the cave and collapsed from exhaustion on the flat stone.

Outside the wind purled and howled, and the rain poured down unremittingly. Darkness fell, and the storm continued to rage throughout the night. The castaway dreamed endlessly of his consort. Theirs was a congress lately consummated in a private Paradise.

As Julian regained consciousness the dim morning light was rising round the summit. At the mouth of the cave he assessed conditions. It was still raining, though the eye of the storm had passed. Amie had not returned during the night, and his heart ached as he thought of her.

Determined to find her, Julian set off down the mountainside. The devastation he saw was overwhelming. With his way often blocked by fallen branches, he painstakingly cleared a path to deliverance. The footing was treacherous and uncertain. Virtually washed away by mud slides and supplementary streams, the remains of the trail challenged even his most persistent effort. A light but consistent rain continued to fall, and it took him the entire morning to reach the Seven Sisters. Along the way he called out at the top of his voice, "Amie! Amie! Amie!"

But no answer reached his ear. Fearing the worst and hoping for a miracle, Julian made his way through the ravaged groves toward Amie's encampment. Coming into the clearing where her house had stood, he could hardly believe the anarchy he witnessed. Crushed, broken and splintered bits the size of tailings were all that remained of her once-proud structure. Certainly swept out to sea when the surge broke upon the shoreline, there was no chance Amie had survived. Her image now faded like a mirage. Julian put his head in his hands and began to sob as the blue and yellow macaw lighted nearby.

"We took shelter in the cave near the cinder cone," Julian explained through his tears. "Before the storm grew so intense, she went down the mountain for food."

"A beacon on an endless sea of time," said BV, eulogizing the light of the forest.

"I cannot imagine life here without her," lamented Julian. "After knowing her, after being here with her, the loneliness will be unbearable. She turned quarantine into Paradise."

"That's the trouble with Paradise," BV said regrettably. "Just when we think it's within our grasp, the scene changes, integrity dissolves, and only fundamentals remain."

"Where is Jewel?" Julian wanted to know.

"Lost," BV croaked. Privation was evident in his voice.

"How?" Julian asked.

"The tree in which we nested toppled. The wash carried it away. I was thrown clear, but Jewel died protecting her eggs."

Fresh tears welled in Julian's eyes. This time he cried for Buenaventura and his mate. He was not sure he could endure such tragedy. He was not certain he could continue. Turning to his friend, Julian suggested they go over the promontory to see if there was anything left of his house or the Scoundrel.

Together they traveled a familiar path. And reaching the summit of the divide, Julian looked down through fog upon the lagoon and beach front. He had expected to see the crushed remnants of his home and his ship, but he saw neither. The strand was totally devoid of debris, as if he had never set foot upon the land, as if he had never put hammer to board and proudly constructed his beach front domicile.

Once on the sandy shore Julian did locate a few of his belongings: his iron winch, pulley and chains were at water's edge; his screwdrivers and wrenches were oddly, but neatly, arranged over a flat stone; and his hammock had torn free of supports and twisted itself round a tree stump.

Amazed to find the Scoundrel beached about one hundred feet inland and pushed up against a line of scrubby trees, Julian walked round and round the boat, carefully inspecting it. Miraculously the craft had sustained only minimal damage. Just how the small boat had avoided destruction remained a mystery.

Turning from the boat, Julian thought he heard a familiar sound. He stopped dead in his tracks. He listened intently as the whir of crackling, sputtering engines grew louder. BV began flapping his wings and chattering delirious nonsense.

"We are running on line. We are running north and south. Will repeat. Will repeat this message on 6210 kcs."

"Not again!" said Julian as he searched the horizon.

"One hundred miles out. Please take bearing and report," said the parrot.

"Where is it, BV?" asked Julian as he searched the sky.

"We are circling but cannot hear you. Go ahead on 7500."

All at once the apparition emerged from low-hanging clouds, trembling as it passed overhead. "The plane!" Julian screamed.

"Merciless life laughs in the burning sun,
And only death intervenes, circling down..."

Buenaventura was nearly convulsive, like an evangelist speaking in tongues. And this time Julian was certain he recognized the pilot's face.

Determined to find the aircraft, he triangulated his position with the plane's angle of descent. Pinpointing the spot where it would land, he started up the hillside through tangled

145

vines and fallen limbs, much as he had his first day on the island. Buenaventura flew branch to branch, all the while uttering nonsense.

Again he reached the fern-covered clearing where he was certain the plane had landed, but saw nothing. A solitary Calico Pennant whirled round and round his head. Following the insect with his eyes, Julian spun himself in a dizzying circle, fascinated in distraction. "Is that you, Amie?" he asked softly.

The dragonfly darted away. Julian sighed. He sat down among the ferns, laughing in the face of futility. Trapped within an experiential loop that seemed to offer no resolution, Julian felt tormented. But perhaps an answer *did* exist to this perpetual riddle...

Directly across the clearing Julian thought he detected a shiny spot covered by the clutter of vines and blades. He moved quickly over the meadow, and reaching the huge object, began removing verdant layers of camouflage. With sweat pouring over his face, he labored with determination. Within minutes the tail, fuselage and cockpit of a long-abandoned plane began to emerge. The words *'Lockheed Electra dural'* were written on the underbelly; the number *NR 16020* was inscribed on the tail.

Julian slithered inside the cockpit. To his surprise the seats were missing. The windshield glass was nowhere in sight. And it appeared that some of the plane's instruments had been purposely removed. On the floor was evidence of dried blood.

He opened the door which led into the fuselage. A putrid smell immediately overwhelmed him. Peering into the tubular chamber and beyond the massive auxiliary fuel tanks, Julian drew a startled breath, then turned away. Confined within the navigator's cabin, the decomposed remains of an individual, now mostly skeletal, lay slumped over a collection of maps and charts.

Stunned and angry, Julian backed out of the cockpit and walked away from the ruined aircraft without turning to look. Such paramount deception had become intolerable. Charging down the mountainside he bellowed out the newly recognized name of one once loved, now despised.

"Amelia! Amelia Earhart! If you ever *were* here, you are long dead. Amie is nothing but your vain attempt at immortality. And I am nothing more than your mirror!" He took the amulet worn round his neck and threw it into the forest.

"I've seen through the glass, Amelia. Paradise cannot be found *or* lost. Paradise is nothing!"

Chapter 4.

When it seems all is lost, what can a man do but begin again? But he must begin slowly, deliberately, re-establishing trust in himself day by day. And though the world has dealt him a crushing blow, he must try to have faith in the world, envisioning a time when all will again be right.

There were things Julian could do, efforts he must make. Or die in his tracks trying. First there was the matter of the dead person. Decency demanded that he have a proper burial, so Julian located Amie's propeller blade shovel before hiking back to the clearing where the camouflaged airplane retained the corpse.

Afraid that lethal bacteria might contaminate his clothing, Julian stripped before crawling back into the fuselage to remove the body. Carrying decomposed flesh and bones over the fuel tanks and out through the cockpit proved to be a wretched struggle, but, again in daylight, Julian laid out the remains near the broken wing of the plane. Then he cleared a place in the ferns for a grave site.

The rain had stopped but the soil was heavy with moisture. Julian talked to Buenaventura as he labored. It took him the entire afternoon to dig the grave, and he buried the man at sunset without a prayer. He placed a smooth stone at the head of the barrow, and upon it he carved a simple epitaph:

> Here lies Fred Noonan
> Navigator of the Electra
> Who made a wrong turn!

"I'm relieved that's finished," he remarked to BV.

Julian walked back to the site of Amie's former home. He was terribly thirsty, and not wanting to put his hands in the stream, he utilized half a coconut shell to drink from a rivulet that flowed from the lower pool of Seven Sisters. Of course he was hungry, too, but the storm had ravaged the fruit trees, and he found precious little to eat. Julian made a torch to light his way, and with BV riding upon his shoulder he walked back over the promontory. There was one more task he needed to perform before resting.

He went straight to the Scoundrel, hoping the containers full of fuel were still on board. Happy to find that they were secure, he hauled one of the cans onto the sand well away from the boat, and bathed himself, head to toe, in gasoline. The fuel burned his skin, but Julian knew that no bacteria would survive such an assault. He lay in the surf for a full hour before putting on his clothes and sleeping upon wet sand.

As morning dawned, he awoke to sunshine. The trade winds were blowing once again, and the glorious bird song he'd grown accustomed to hearing at sunrise filled spaces so recently left empty by artifice. Though today he had no time to lament. He had much work to do.

Upon a bit of driftwood Buenaventura laid an array of seeds and fruits, which he had gathered during the night for his companion. Julian found the gift and nourished himself. BV perched nearby and watched with satisfaction.

Julian's first task was to collect as many of his possessions as possible, especially his tools. To that end he made a semi-circle through the windswept vegetation across an upland radius of half a mile. During the course of the morning he found his water containers, his fishing rods and nets, three buckets, a knife, his first aid kit, some cookware, a long piece of rope, his canvas tarp, and the cardboard tube in which he'd stored his collection of nautical maps. On the beach he laid out his recovered possessions.

Wrapping his mechanic's tools in a homemade sling, he went up the mountainside to the place where the *Electra* lay shrouded in mystery. Reaching the airplane, he began stripping away the remaining vines and creepers, finally exposing the entire length of the battered and broken aircraft. Over the years much of the casing had rusted, but the cowling that covered the wings and engines still shone bright silver in the afternoon sun. From wreckage and debris Julian made a platform on which to stand. He tried to loosen the bolts that held a protective sheath over the internal engine works. Evidently, they were corroded shut. A well-placed blow with his hammer managed to loosen two of the rusted bolts, and he muscled the cover free. With intense curiosity he examined the Lockheed's engines.

Julian was certainly no mechanic. Not yet, anyway. But a motor was a motor, was it not? And any fool could see that the *Electra's* Pratt & Whitney Wasp engines were not appreciably different from those which powered the Scoundrel. Removing the air filter housing, he exposed the carburetors and examined the fuel intake jets. Their configuration was not quite identical to those of the Scoundrel's inboard engines; but, he speculated, with a little creative modification perhaps certain fundamental parts might somehow be adapted to repair the Scoundrel's impaired engines. He certainly meant to try.

Disassembling the two carburetors Julian was careful not to mislay a single spring or screw. For he knew each part might prove crucial in his bid for escape. At each stage of the operation he drew a schematic on the palm of his hand. There could be no tolerance for ignorance, no substitute for accuracy.

"Of course this is lunacy," Julian told himself. "How can it possibly work?" Unwilling to trust even his skepticism, he crawled again into the *Electra's* fuselage to retrieve Noonan's charts, his sextant, and his drift indicator.

And with incessant hunger cramping his stomach, and sweat drenching his face and half-naked body, Julian worked sunup till sundown with single-minded determination. "I have never fully understood the properties of an internal combustion engine," he acknowledged. "But I can learn. I *will* learn!"

With an assortment of engine parts bound in the cloth sling, Julian started back down the mountain. Ever since the storm Buenaventura had not left his side. Again this evening Julian stopped near the Seven Sisters for water. He was hungry - especially for protein. Fondly remembering the taste of Amie's turtle stew, he stared at the disarranged remnants of her domicile. Amelia's last home...

Julian might have allowed himself to question the meaning of his unlikely encounter with the lost aviatrix, but sensing a metaphysical trap, he stopped himself. Such an assessment would have to wait until his environment was more stable. If ever that were to happen...

At present his efforts were methodical. And meticulous. He meant to dismantle not only four dormant engines, but the entire disposition of his remarkable circumstance. He would study each element, determine purpose, assure function. And he knew that he alone was the source from which redemption might emanate.

That night he fished for his supper with little success. He caught sand crabs in the twilight, ate bitter greens, sucked the juice from a split rind. He tried in vain to slake his thirst with cupful after cupful of water collected from the Seven Sisters' stream. At the edge of forever, his dreams were not of Amie - nor of Amelia Earhart - but of Kelly and Kirsten.

Next morning Julian tinkered endlessly with the Scoundrel's carburetors - substituting, improvising, re-conforming. Having assembled what seemed to be an integrated system, there was, in the end, no way to test re-invention, for it was impossible to start the engines with the boat beached upon the sand. Confronted with the monumental problem of how to move the Scoundrel off the beach and back into the water, Julian knew he was not strong enough to push, pull, or drag the cruiser

151

even one foot, let alone one hundred feet or more! Perhaps there was another answer. His winch and pulley, along with yards of chain that had once secured his lost anchor, now promised uncertain deliverance. If only he could devise a method of fastening the winch to an immovable object offshore.

Looking out to sea, Julian remarked, "That's a helluva lot of water..."

"*Sure thing, brother,*" laughed Kong. "*And that's just the top of it!*"

True, there was nothing atop. But what about below, he asked himself? If he was able to drive spikes into the coral as a makeshift anchor to secure the boat, then why not go below and attach the winch that way as well? Levers could be employed to turn the ship. Perhaps ramps, too. Or even rollers. After all, the beach *did* slope toward the water. And the winch and pulley would clearly function beneath the surface...

For the first time since his dive off Molokini Island, Julian donned the scuba gear. He swam out to the coral reef and went below to assess the potential of his plan. Before the afternoon light had gone he was driving spikes into the coral to serve as support for the winch.

Next day Julian spent connecting chain link to the boat's prow and attaching the winch and pulley to the newly fashioned, underwater grapnel. Calling up all his strength, he cinched the remaining slack from the chain, then came out of the water to begin inserting wedges cut from tree limbs underneath the boat. With these he might inch the cruiser forward, then stabilize the new position by tightening the chain with the winch and pulley. Certainly the process would be arduous. Progress would have to be measured in inches gained. But in time Julian was sure he could move the boat back into the water. His determination and his will would compound his physical strength. "This boat *will* reach the water!" he insisted. "I *will* move it!"

Two weeks' labor: half the distance covered. No doubt the system worked, but Julian's strength was failing by the day. Fishing was poor; he was living on nuts and berries gathered by Buenaventura. Grateful for whatever provisions his loyal friend might provide, the man was, nevertheless, slowly starving. But he would not give up! Each day he positioned the wedges, then put on the scuba gear and swam out to tighten the towing chain. Back on shore he gave every last bit of strength to the task of prying the boat forward, inch by painstaking inch. Exhausted, Julian finally collapsed face down on the sand, where he lay nearly an hour. Summoning reserves from a source where none should have remained, he put his shoulder to the task again. And again.

Twenty-five days passed, and the Scoundrel now rested at the periphery of sand and sea. One decisive effort and the seemingly impossible chore of moving the boat off dry land and back into the water would be accomplished. Julian resolved not to desist until the Scoundrel was afloat again, and he swam out to the winch intent on moving the huge cruiser the final few feet necessary for buoyancy.

But as he moved the crank of the winch forward and fixed the ratchet in place, the chain groaned under the strain. One notch tighter, and it snapped with a fierce recoil. "No! No!" Julian screamed as he held the severed chain link in his hand.

Frying a small fish over an open driftwood fire at sunset, the castaway's dejection was evident. The once immutable look of determination was now absent from his face. His posture had gone slack. His vision grew dim. An entire month's labor wasted, and possibly his last real hope of reconvening his contracted life lost, he felt utterly defeated.

Assessing the disparity of his situation, he turned to BV and moaned, "I don't want to remain here. I want to go home. But it's no use. With the Scoundrel dry docked, I can't leave. And no matter how long I'm stranded here, I will never begin to approach the balance which Amelia was able to create."

"What balance?" Buenaventura derided. "Her legacy is eternal enigma."

"Perhaps time does not really exist until the moment of death," Julian premised. "Within this succession of days and years, within this realm of joy and sorrow, perspective is impossible."

"And maybe that's the human condition," said BV. "Could be the struggle for redemption is programmed into your DNA."

That night seemed very long indeed.

Morning dawned in gray light, and Julian awoke to the sound of copious waves breaking onshore. Shortly thereafter it began to rain, though the intensity of this storm was unlike Wili-Wili. The frequency and height of the waves reminded him of the storm that had first brought him to the island. At the time landfall seemed to be the very redemption he now regarded with unequivocal contempt. Again he used the canvas tarp to build a lean-to on the beach.

The rain fell steadily and the incoming waves grew larger throughout the morning. At first, Julian perceived the rainstorm to be yet another assault upon his comfort and well being. But as he watched the swells roll over the reef and break upon the shore, a new sense of hope and possibility issued from deep within his humanity.

The Scoundrel now rocked with the denouement of each ten-foot curl. It's movements toward the water seemed imperceptible at first, but grew incrementally more obvious as the tide increased. Julian could barely believe his eyes. The progress that surely would have involved another week's work had the towing chain held out was being accomplished in minutes by the pounding surf.

Julian ran down the beach to where his boat was still aground. Between breakers he examined indentations near the ship's stern. Marks in the wet sand confirmed his impression. The boat was definitely moving toward the water. Shrieking with delight Julian ran for safety as the next pipeline thundered ashore. Turning back, he watched as the mighty crests pummeled ship and shoreline. The Scoundrel inched forward again. With each wave he came closer to hegira. Julian begged aloud for the storm to continue. And when the penultimate foamy wave crashed ashore, the Scoundrel at last broke ground and bobbed freely in the shallow waters of the cove.

When the rain finally quit, Julian waded into the lagoon and climbed on board the Scoundrel. He poured fuel into the gas tanks, primed the carburetors, and checked to make sure the blades cleared bottom. Overhead the sound of airborne engines faltered amidst dense cloud cover, but this time Julian paid no attention. Succeed or fail, he had to know if his modifications would indeed power the cruiser. Indulging no reticence, he turned the ignition key and held his breath. The inboards roared back to life, and the reinstated sailor danced happily on deck.

"Buenaventura!" he called. "Are you staying here, or coming with me?"

BV abandoned Paradise and flew to his perch on board the Scoundrel.

From the head Julian throttled up the engines and took the cruiser out of the cove. As the island receded, he recalled the landing at Hilo Harbor of the voyaging canoe, *Hawai'iloa*. Julian considered Nainoa Nainoa's prodigious accomplishment. Without a motor to power his boat the venturous sailor had traveled all the way from the Marquesas to Hawaii. Perhaps he, too, might discover within himself the vision to navigate the broad expanse of water between Paradise and a place called home.

Chapter 5.

He sailed into the small boat harbor at Lahaina without a welcome. Exhausted, malnourished and dehydrated, Julian had successfully traveled the tenuous lane between the Empyrean and earthly life. Mooring the Scoundrel in slip number thirteen, he stepped onto the Lahaina pier. The place looked as though he had left only yesterday. But perhaps it was yesterday.

He left the pier and walked up Front Street with BV riding upon his shoulder. With skin the color of cinnamon and dressed only in filthy tattered shorts and sennit rope sandals, with sun-bleached beard woolly and full, and his hair tangled and tied into a pony tail, Julian must have resembled a pirate in port as he passed the Carthaginian sailing ship and the Pioneer Inn.

Still possessing the key to Kevin Miles' apartment, he went directly there to attend his personal needs. For three days he secluded himself, neither seeing nor talking to anyone. He rested and nourished himself. He shaved off his beard and tenderly combed out his snarled hair. He cherished the feel of fresh clothing on his body. He found the taste of tap water quite peculiar. Television made him feel tense. Street noise was invasive. The support of a real bed was unaccustomed. He felt dissociated, nevertheless happy to be back.

"I miss Amie," Julian confessed to BV. "I suppose you miss Jewel, too."

"These experiences are within us now," the parrot told him. "Like Amelia's myth, they will last forever..."

On his fourth day back in Lahaina, Julian ventured out of Miles' apartment. Intent on documenting his appearance at the end of the ordeal, he visited a photography studio where he had a portrait of himself made. A broken front tooth distinguished his shy smile.

Next morning he walked up Front Street to the Sunrise Cafe. Buenaventura perched upon his shoulder. At the cafe's counter Song Cajudoy greeted him as if he'd been there only yesterday. Kamehaloha Kong sat idly at his usual table, a glass of POG before him.

Julian approached Kong's table and took a seat.

"*Aloha*, little brother," said Kamehaloha. "I saw the Scoundrel docked at slip number thirteen, so I knew you were back in town."

"It was quite a trip," said Julian.

"I see you made it through Wili-Wili."

"Thanks for the note," said Julian.

"And how is my ship sailing?" Kong wanted to know.

"Well, I had a little trouble with the carburetors, you know. But I managed to re-jet the intake valves with some spare parts I came upon, and now the engines are running well."

Kamehaloha smiled. "So, what's next?" said Kong as he sipped his juice.

"First off," said Julian, "I'm giving the Scoundrel back to you, Kamehaloha."

"I can't refund your money, brother."

"I think I got more than my money's worth," said Julian. The Scoundrel took me places no other boat could have taken me."

"Are you certain you want to give it up?" Kong asked.

"I've decided to go back to California," Julian related.

"Oblivion in California!" screamed BV.

157

Kong laughed heartily at the bird's assessment. He turned to Julian and asked, "What are you going to do with him? The Department of Agriculture will never allow you to export a parrot."

"My one regret," said Julian. "I was hoping that Song would keep him here at the Sunrise."

"Where's Julian?" called BV. "*Electra* is running on line. Will repeat. Will repeat..."

Song also laughed at the bird's antics. "Buenaventura will always have a home here," the Filipina promised.

"Life at the Sunrise... What a Paradise!" proclaimed BV.

"When are you leaving, Julian?" Kamehaloha asked.

"I fly home day after tomorrow," Julian informed.

"You won't forget us, here at the Sunrise..."

"No chance of that," said Julian. "And just so you won't forget me, I had this photo of myself taken. I'd be honored, Song, if it hung here at the Sunrise right next to Kamehaloha's picture."

"Thank you, Julian," said Song. "I'll hang it up right now."

Hammer and tack in hand, Song noticed that Julian had written a rather curious caption at the bottom of the 8X10 black and white photograph. It read:

"Paradise... Just when we think it's within our grasp, the scene changes, integrity dissolves, and only fundamentals remain."

The day after Julian left for California, Tamara Sly walked into the Sunrise Cafe. From his perch in the rafters BV called out, "Tamara Sly! Tomorrow's lie"

"Where did he come from?" the beach girl wanted to know.

Song winked at BV. "Julian Crosby showed up a few days ago and left him here. I foolishly agreed to adopt him."

"Where is Julian staying? On the Scoundrel?"

"No, he gave the cruiser back to Kamehaloha. Julian went back to California," said Song.

"Too bad I missed him. I would have liked to wish him well," said Tamara. She ordered her usual passion fruit cocktail and sat down at the counter. Her sarong fell away from her bare thigh. "Where's Kamehaloha?" she asked.

"He's down at the small boat launch adjusting the carburetors on the Scoundrel's engines," said Song. "I think he means to sell it. Again."

"Oh," said Tamara. "Well, when you see him, tell him there's a *haole* in town looking for him..."